D1806090

A Family Affair and Other Short Stories

Kate Chopin

78 H   CHOP

1 021

03

Colchester VI Form College

00031021

CONTENTS

A Family Affair

1899

The moment that the wagon rattled out of the yard away to the station, Madame Solisainte settled herself into a state of nervous expectancy.

She was superabundantly fat; and her body accommodated itself to the huge chair in which she sat, filling up curves and crevices like water poured into a mould. She was clad in an ample muslin *peignoir* sprigged with brown. Her cheeks were flabby, her mouth thin-lipped and decisive. Her eyes were small, watchful, and at the same time timid. Her brown hair, streaked with gray, was arranged in a bygone fashion, a narrow mesh being drawn back from the centre of the forehead to conceal a bald spot, and the sides plastered down smooth over her small, close ears.

The room in which she sat was large and uncarpeted. There were handsome and massive pieces of furniture decorating the apartment, and a magnificent brass clock stood on the mantelpiece.

Madame Solisainte sat at a back window which overlooked the yard, the brick kitchen – a little removed from the house – and the field road which led down to the negro quarters. She was unable to leave her chair. It was an affair of importance to get her out of bed in the morning, and an equally arduous task to put her back there at night.

It was a sore affliction to the old woman to be thus incapacitated during her latter years, and rendered unable to watch and control her household affairs. She was sure that she was being robbed continuously and on all sides. This conviction was nourished and kept alive by her confidential servant Dimple, a very black girl of sixteen, who trod softly about on her bare feet and had thereby made her self unpopular in the kitchen and down at the quarters.

The notion had entered Madame Solisainte's head to have one of her neices come up from New Orleans and stay with her. She thought it would be doing the niece and her family a great kindness, and would furthermore be an incalculable saving to herself in many ways, and far cheaper than hiring a housekeeper.

There were four nieces, not too well off, with whom she was indifferently acquainted. In selecting one of these to make her home on the plantation she exercised no choice, leaving that matter to her sister and the girls, to be settled among them.

It was Bosey who consented to go to her aunt. Her mother spelled her name Bosé. She herself spelled it Bosey. But as often as not she was called plain Bose. It was she who was sent, because, as her mother wrote to Madame Solisainte, Bosé was a splendid manager, a most excellent housekeeper, and moreover possessed a tempermant of such rare amiablilty that none could help being cheered and enlivened by her presence.

What she did not write was that none of the other girls would entertain the notion for an instant of making even a temporary abiding place with their *Tante* Félicie. And Bosey's consent was only wrung from her with the understanding that the undertaking was purely experimental, and that she bound herself by no cast-iron obligations.

Madame Solisainte had sent the wagon to the station for her neice, and was impatiently awaiting its return. "It's no sign of the wagon yet, Dimple? You don't see it? You don't year it coming?"

"No'um; 'tain't no sign. De train des 'bout lef' de station. I yeard it w'istle." Dimple stood on the back porch beside her mistress' open window. She wore a calico dress so skimp and inadequate that her growing figure was bursting through the rents and apertures. She was constantly pinning it at the back of the waist with a bent safety-pin which was forever giving way. The task of pinning her dress and biting the old brass safety-pin into shape occupied a great deal of her time.

"It's true," Madame said. "I recommend to Daniel to drive those mule' very slow in this how weather. They are not strong, those mule'."

"He drive 'em slow 'nough long's he's in the fiel' road!" exclaimed Dimple. "Time he git roun'in de big road whar you kain't see 'im – uh! uh! he make' dem mule' fa'r' lope!"

Madame tightened her lips and blinked her eyes. She rarely replied otherwise to these disclosures of Dimple, but they sank into her soul and festered there.

The cook – in reality a big-boned field hand – came in with pans and pails to get out the things for supper. Madame kept her provisions right there under her nose in a large closet, or cupboard, which she had had built in the side of the room. A small supply of butter was in a jar that stood on the hearth, and the eggs were kept in a basket that hung on a peg near by.

Dimple came in and unlocked the cupboard, taking the keys from her mistress' bag. She gave out a little flour, a little meal, a cupful of coffee, some sugar and a piece of bacon. Four eggs were wanted for a pudding, but Madame thought that two would be enough, finally compromising, however, upon three.

Miss Bosey Brantonniere arrived at her aunt's house with three trunks, a large, circular, tin bathtub, a bundle of umbrellas and sunshades, and a small dog. She was a pretty, energetic-looking girl, with her chin in the air, tastefully dressed in the latest fashion, and dispersing an atmosphere of bustle and importance about her. Daniel had driven her up the field road, depositing her at the back entrance, where Madame, from her window, commanded a complete view of her arrival.

"I thought you would have sent the carriage for me, *Tante* Félicie, but Daniel tells me you have no carriage," said the girl after the first greetings were over. She had had her trunks taken to her room, the tub slipped under the bed, and now she sat fondling the dog and talking to *Tante* Félicie.

The old lady shook her head dismally and her lips curled into a disparaging smile.

"Oh! no, no! The ol' carriage 'as been sol' ages ago to Zéphire Lablatte. It was falling to piece' in the shed. Me – I never stir f'um w'ere you see me; it is good two year' since 'ave been inside the church, let alone to go *en promenade*."

"Well, I'm going to take all care and bother off your shoulders, *Tante* Félicie," uttered the girl cheerfully. "I'm going to brighten things up for you, and we'll see how quickly you'll improve. Why, in less than two months I'll have you on your feet, going about as spry as anybody."

Madame was far less hopeful. "My ol' mother was the same," she replied with dejected resignation. "Nothing could 'elp her. She lived many year' like you see me; your mamma mus' 'ave often tol' you."

Mrs. Brantonniere had never related to the girls anything disparaging concerning their Aunt Félicie, but other members of the family had been less considerate, and Bosey had often been told of her aunt's avarice and grasping ways. How she had laid her clutch upon her mother's belongings, taking undisputed possession by the force of audacity alone. The girl could not help thinking it must have been while her grandmother sat so helpless in her huge chair that *Tante* Félicie had made herself mistress of the situation. But she was not one to harbor malice. She felt very sorry for *Tante* Félicie, so afflicted in her childless old age.

Madame lay long awake that night troubled someway over the advent of this niece from New Orleans, who was not precisely what she had expected. She did not like the excess of trunks, the bathtub and the dog, all of which indicated determination and promised trouble. Dimple was warned next morning to say nothing to her mistress concerning a surprise which Miss Bosey had in store for her. This surprise was that, instead of being deposited in her accustomed place at the back window, where she could keep an eye upon her people, Madame was installed at the front-room window that looked out toward the live oaks and along a leafy, sleepy road that was seldom used.

"*Jamais! Jamais!* it will never do! *Pas possible!*" cried out the old lady with helpless excitement when she perceived what was about to be done to her.

"You'll do just as I say, *Tante* Félicie," said Bosey, with sprightly determination. "I'm here to take care of you and make you comfortable, and I'm going to do it. Now, instead of looking out on that hideous back yard, full of dirty little darkies, and pigs and chickens wallowing round, here you have this sweet, peaceful view whenever you look out of the window. Now, here comes Dimple with the magazines and things. Bring them right here, Dimple, and lay them on the table beside Ma'me Félicie. I brought these up from the city expressly for you, *Tante*, and I have a whole trunkful more when you are through with them."

Dimple was entering, staggering with arms full of books and periodicals of all sizes, shapes and colors. The strain of carrying the weight of literature had caused the safety-pin to give way, and Dimple feared it might have fallen and been lost.

"So, *Tante* Félicie, you'll have nothing to do but read and enjoy yourself. Here are some French books mamma sent you, something by Daudet, something by Maupassant and a lot more. Here, let me brighten up your spectacles." She brightened the old lady's glasses with a piece of thin tissue paper which fell from one of the books.

"And now, Madame Solisainte, you give me all the keys! Turn them right over, and I'll go out and make myself thoroughly acquainted with everything." Madame spasmodically clutched the bag that swung to the arm of her chair.

"Oh! a whole bagful!" exclaimed the girl, gently but firmly disengaging it from her aunt's claw-like fingers. "My, what an undertaking I have before me! Dimple had better show me round this morning until I get thoroughly acquainted. You can knock on the door with your stick when you want her. Come along, Dimple. Fasten your dress." The girl was scanning the floor for the safety-pin, which she found out in the hall.

During all of Madame Solisainte's days no one had ever spoken to her with the authority which this young woman assumed. She did not know what to make of it. She felt that she should have revolted at once against being thus banished to the front room. She should have spoken out and maintained possession of her keys when demanded, with the spirit of a highway robber, to give them up. She pounded her stick on the floor with loud and sudden energy. Dimple appeared with inquisitive eyes.

"Dimple," said Madame, "tell Miss Bosé to please 'ave the kin'ness an sen'me back my bag of key'."

Dimple vanished and returned almost on the instant.

5

"Miss Bosey 'low don't you bodda. Des you go on lookin' at de picters. She ain' gwine let nuttin' happen to de keys."

After an uneasy interval Madame recalled the girl.

"Dimple, if you could look in the bag an' bring me my armoire key – you know it – the brass one. Do not let on as though I would want that key in partic'lar."

"De bag hangin' on her arm. She got de string twis' roun' her wris'," reported Dimple presently. Madame Félicie inwardly fumed with impotent rage.

"W'at is she doing, Dimple?" she asked uneasily.

"She got de cubbud do's fling wide open. She standin' on a cha'r lookin' in de corners an' behin' eve'ything."

"Dimple!" called out Bosey from the far room. And away flew Dimple, who had not been so pleasingly agitated since the previous Christmas.

After a little while, of her own accord she stole noiselessly back into the room where Madame Félicie sat in speechless wrath beside the table of books. She closed the door behind her, rolled her eyes, and spoke in a hoarse whisper:

"She done fling 'way de barrel o' meal; 'low it all fill up wid weevils."

"Weevil'!" cried out her mistress.

"Yas'um, weevils; 'low it plumb sp'ilt. 'Low it on'y fitten fo' de chickens an' hogs; 'tain't fitten fo' folks. She done make Dan'el roll it out on de gal'ry."

"Weevil'!" reiterated Madame Félicie, tremulous with suppressed excitement. "Bring me some of that meal in a saucer, Dimple. Don't let on anything."

She and Dimple bent over the cup of meal which the girl brought concealed under her skirt.

"Do you see any weevil', you, Dimple?"

"No'um." Dimple smelled it, and Madame felt the sample of meal and rolled a pinch or two between her fingers. It was lumpy, musty and old.

"She got Susan out dah helpin' her," insinuated Dimple, "an' Sam an' Dan'el; all helpin' her."

"*Bon Dieu!* It won't be a grain of sugar left, a bar of soap – nothing! nothing! Go watch, Dimple. Don't stan' there like a stick."

"She 'low she gwine sen' Susan back to wuk in de fiel'," went on Dimple, heedless of her mistress' admonition. "She 'low Susan don' know how to cook. Susan say she willin' to go back, her. An' Miss Bosey, she ax Dan'el ef he know a fus'-class cook, w'at kin brile chicken an' steak an' make good soup, an' waffles, an' rolls, an fricassee, an' dessert, an' custud, an sich."

She passed her tongue over a slobbering lip. "Dan'el say his wife Mandy done cook fo' de pa'tic'lest people in town, but she don' wuk cheap 'nough fo' Ma'me Félicie. An' Miss Bosey, she 'low it don' make no odd' 'bout de price, 'long she git hole somebody w'at know how to cook."

Madame's fingers worked nervously at the illuminated cover of a magazine. She said nothing. Only tightened her lips and blinked her small eyes.

When Bosey thrust her head in at the door to inquire how "*Tantine*" was getting on, the old lady fumbled at the books with a pretense of having been occupied with looking at them.

"That's right, *Tante* Félicie! You look as comfortable as can be. I wanted to make you a nice glass of lemonade, but Susan tells me there isn't a lemon on the place. I told Fannie's boy to bring up half a box of lemons from Lablatte's store in the handcart. There's nothing healthier than lemonade in summer. And he's going to bring a chunk of icc, too. We'll have to order ice from town after this." She had on a white apron over her gingham dress, and her sleeves were rolled to the elbows.

"I detes' lemonade; it is bad for *mon estomac*," interposed Madame vehemently. "We 'ave no use in the worl' for lemon', an' there is no place vere to keep ice. Tell Fannie's boy never min' about lemon' an' ice."

"Oh, he's gone long ago! And as for the ice, why, Daniel says he can make me a box lined with sawdust – he made one for Doctor Godfrey. We can keep it under the back porch." And away she went, the embodiment of the throughgoing, bustling little housewife. Somewhat past noon, Dimple came in with an air of importance, removed the books, and spread a white damask cloth upon the table. It was like spreading a red cloth before a sullen bull. Madame's eyes glared at the cloth.

"W'ere did you get that?" she asked as if she would have annihilated Dimple on the spot.

"Miss Bosey, she tuck it out de big press; tuck some mo' out; 'low she kain't eat on dat meal-sack w'at we alls calls de table-clot'e." The damask cloth bore the initials of Madame's mother, embroidered in a corner.

"She done kilt two dem young pullets in de *basse-cour*," went on Dimple, like a croaking raven. "Mandy come lopin' up f'om de quarters time Dan'el told 'er. She yonder, rarin' roun' in de kitchen. Dey done sent fo' some sto' lard an' bakin' powders down to Lablatte's. Fannie's boy, he ben totin' all mornin'. De cubbad done look lak a sto'."

"Dimple!" called Bosey in the distance.

When she returned it was with a pompous air, her head uplifted, and stepping carefully like a fat chicken. She bore a tray weighted with a repast such as she had never before in her life served to Madame Solisainte.

Mandy had outdone herself. She had broiled the breast of a pullet to a turn. She had fried the potatoes after a New Orleans receipt, and had made a pudding of richest ingredients of her own invention which had given her a name in the parish. There were two milky-looking poached eggs, and the biscuits were as light as snowflakes and the color of gold. The forks and spoons were of massive silver, also bearing the initials of Madame's mother. They had been reclaimed from the press with the table linen.

Under this new, strange influence Madame Solisainte seemed to have been deprived of the power of asserting her will. There was an occasional outburst like the flare of a smouldering fire, but she was outwardly timid and submissive. Only when she was alone with her young handmaid did she speak her mind.

Bosey took special care in arranging her aunt's toilet one morning not long after her arrival. She fastened a sheer white 'kerchief (which she found in the press) about the old lady's neck. She powdered her face from her own box of *duvet de cygnet*; and she gave her a fine linen handkerchief (which she also found in the press), sprinkling it from the bottle of cologne water which she had brought from New Orleans. She filled the vase upon the table with fresh flowers, and dusted and rearranged the books there.

Madame had been moving forward the bookmark in the novel to pretend that she was reading it.

These unusual preparations were explained an hour or two later, when Bosey introduced into Madame Solisainte's presence their neighbor, Doctor Godfrey. He was a youngish, good-looking man, with a loud, cheery voice and a super-abundance of animal spirits. He seemed to carry about with him the very atmosphere of health and to dispense it broadcast in invisible waves.

"Do you see, *Tante* Félicie, how I think of everything? When I saw, last night, the suffering you endured at being put to bed, I decided that you ought to be under a physician's treatment. So the first thing I did this morning was to send a messenger for Doctor Godfrey, and here he is!"

Madame glared at him as he drew up a chair on the opposite side of the table and began to talk about how long it was since he had seen her. "I do not need a physician!" she cried in tones of exasperation, looking from one to the other. "All the physician' in the worl' cannot 'elp me. My mother was the same; she try all the physician' of the parish. She went to the 'ot spring', to *la Nouvelle Orleans,* an' she die at las' in this chair. Nothing will 'elp me."

"That is for me to say, Madame Solisainte," said the Doctor with cheerful assurance. "It is a good idea of your niece's that you should place yourself under a physician's care. I don't say mine, understand – there are many excellent physicians in the parish – but some one ought to look after you, if it is only to keep you in comfortable condition."

Madame blinked at him under lowered brows. She was thinking of his bill for this visit, and determined that he should not make a second one. She saw ruin staring her in the face, and felt as if she were being borne along on a raging torrent of extravagance to meet it.

Bosey had already explained Madame's symptoms to the Doctor, and he said he would send or bring over a preparation which Madame Solisainte must take night and morning till he saw fit to alter or discontinue it. Then he glanced at the magazines, while he and the girl engaged in a lively conversation across Madame's chair. His eyes sparkled with animation as he looked at Bosey, as fresh and sweet in her pink dimity gown as one of the flowers there on the table.

He came very often, and Madame grew sick with apprehension and uncertainty, unable to distinguish between his professional and social visits. At first she refused to take his medicine until Bosey stood over her one evening with a spoonful, gently but firmly expressing a determination to stand there till morning, if necessary, and Madame consented to swallow the mixture. The Doctor took Bosey out driving in his new buggy behind two fast trotters. The first time, after she had driven away, Madam Félicie charged Dimple to go into Miss Bosey's room and search everywhere for the bag of keys. But they were not to be found.

"She mus' kiard 'em wid 'er. She all time got 'em twis' roun' 'er arm. I believe she sleep wid' 'em twis' roun' 'er arm," offered Dimple in explanation of her failure.

Unable to find the keys, she turned to examining the young girl's dainty belongings – such as were not under lock. She crept back into

Madame Félicie's room, carrying a lace-filled parasol which she silently held out for Madame's inspection. The lace was simple and inexpensive, but the old woman shuddered at sight of it as if it had been the rarest of d'Alençon.

Perceiving the impression created by the gay sunshade, Dimple next brought in a pair of slippers with spangled toes, a fine pair of stockings that hung on the back of a chair, an embroidered petticoat, and finally a silk waist. She brought the articles one by one, with a certain solemnity rendered doubly impressive by her silence.

Dimple was wearing her best dress – a red calico with ruffles and puffed sleeves (Miss Bosey had compelled her to discard the other). As a consequence of this holiday attire Dimple gave herself Sunday airs, and passed her time hanging to the gallery post or doubling her body across the bannister rail.

Bosey grew more and more prolific in devices for her Aunt Félicie's comfort and entertainment. She invited Madame's old friends to visit her, singly and in groups; to spend the day – in some instances several days.

She began to have company herself. The young gentlemen and girls of the parish came from miles around to pay their respects. She was of a hospitable turn, and dispensed iced lemonade on such occasions, and sangaree – Lablatte having ordered a case of red wine form the city. There was constant baking of cakes going on in the kitchen, Daniel's wife surpassing all her former efforts in that direction.

Bosey gave lawn parties, with the Chinese lanterns all festooned among the oaks, with three musicians from the quarters playing the fiddle, the guitar and accordion on the gallery, right under Madame Solisainte's nose. She gave a ball and dressed *Tante* Félicie up for the occasion in a silk peignoir which she had had made in the city as a surprise.

The Doctor took Bosey driving or horseback riding every other day. He all but lived at Madame Solisainte's, and was in danger of losing all his practice, till Bosey, in mercy, promised to marry him.

She kept her engagement a secret from *Tante* Félicie, pursuing her avocation of the ministering angel up to the very day of her departure for the city to make preparations for her approaching marriage.

A beatitude, a beneficent joy settled upon Madame when Bosey announced her engagement to the Doctor and her intention to leave the plantation that afternoon.

"Oh! You can't imagine, *Tante* Félicie, how I regret to leave you – just as I was getting things so comfortably and pleasantly settled about you, too. If you want, perhaps Fifine or sister Adèle would come –"

"No! no!" cried Madame in shrill protest. "Nothing of the kin'! I insist, let them stay w'ere they are. I am ole; I am use' to my ways. It is not 'ard for me to be alone. I will not year of it!"

Madame could have sung for very joy as she listened all morning to the bustle of her niece's packing. She even petted doggie in her exuberance, for she had aimed many a blow at him with her stick when he had had the temerity to trust himself alone with her. The trunks and the bathtub were sent away at noon. The clatter accompanying their departure sounded like sweet music in Madame Solisainte's ears. It was with almost feeling of affection that she embraced her niece when the girl came and kissed her good-by. The Doctor was going to drive his *fiancèe* to the station in his buggy.

He told Madame Félicie that he felt like an archangel. In reality, he looked demented with happiness and excitement. She was as sauve as honey to him. She was thinking that in the character of a nephew he would not have the indelicacy to present a bill for professional services.

The Doctor hurried out to turn the horses and to get ready the lap-robe to spread over the knees of his divinity. Bosey looked as dainty as the day she had made her appearance, in the same brown linen gown and jaunty traveling hat. There was a fathomless look in her blue eyes.

"And now, *Tante* Félicie," she said finally, "here is your bag of keys. You will find everything in perfect order, and I hope you will be satisfied. All the purchases have been entered in the book – you will find Lablatte's bills and everything correct. But, by the way, *Tante Félicie*, I want to tell you – I have made an equal division of grandmother's silver and table linen and jewels which I found in the strong box, and sent them to mamma. You know yourself it was only just; mamma had as much right to them as you. So, good-by, *Tante Félicie*. You are quite sure you wouldn't like to have sister Adèle?"

"*Voleuse! voleuse! voleuse!*" she heard her aunt's voice lifted after her in a shrill scream. It followed her as far as the leafy road beyond the live oaks.

Madame Solisainte trembled with excitement and agitation. She looked into the bag and counted the keys. They were all there.

"*Voleuse!*" she kept muttering. She was convinced that Bosey had robbed her of everything she possessed. The jewels were gone, she was sure of it – all gone. Her mother's watch and chain; bracelets, rings, ear-rings, everything gone. All the silver; the table, the bed linen, her mother's clothes – ah! that was why she had brought those three trunks!

Madame Solisainte clutched the brass key and glared at it with eyes wild with apprehension. She pounded her stick upon the floor till the rafters rang. But at that time of the afternoon – the hours between dinner and supper – the yard was deserted. And Dimple, still under the delusion created by the red ruffles and puffed sleeves, was strolling leisurely toward the station to see Miss Bosey off.

Madame pounded and called. In her wrath she overturned the table and sent the books and magazines flying in all directions. She sat a while a prey to the most violent agitation, the most turbulent misgivings, that made the pulses throb in her head and the blood course through her body as though the devil himself were at the valve.

"Robbed! Robbed! Robbed!" she repeated. "My gold; the rings; the necklace! I might have known! Oh! fool! Ah! *cher maître! pas possible!*"

Her head quivered as with a palsy upon its fat bulk. She clutched the arm of her chair and attempted to rise; her effort was fruitless. A second attempt, and she drew herself a few inches out of the chair and fell back again. A third effort, in which her whole big body shook and swayed like a vessel which has sprung a leak, and Madame Solisainte stood upon her feet.

She grasped the cane there at hand and stood helpless, screaming for Dimple. Then she began to walk – or rather drag her feet along the floor, slowly and with painful effort, shaking and leaning heavily upon her stick.

Madame did not think it strange or miraculous that she should be moving thus upon her tottering limbs, which for two years had refused to do their office. Her whole attention was bent upon reaching the press in her bedroom across the hall. She clutched the brass key; she had let all the other keys go, and she said nothing now but *"Volè, volè, volè!"*

Madame Solisainte managed to reach the room without other assistance than the chairs in her way afforded her, and the walls along which she propped her body as she sidled along. Her first thought upon unlocking the press was for her gold. Yes, there it was, all of it, in little piles as she had so often arranged it. But half the silver was gone; half the jewels and table linen.

When the servants began to congregate in the yard, they discovered Madame Fèlicie standing upon the gallery waiting for them. They uttered exclamations of wonder and consternation. Dimple became hysterical, and began to cry and scream out.

"Go an' fin' Richmond," said Madame to Daniel, and without comment or question he hurried off in search of the overseer.

"I will 'ave the law! Ah! *par example! pas possible!* to be rob' in that way! I will 'ave the law. Tell Lablatte I will not pay the bills. Mandy, go back the the quarters, an' sen' Susan to the kitchen. Dimple! Go an' carry all those book' an' magazine' up in the attic, an' put on you' other dress. Do not let me fin' you array in those flounce' again! *Pas possible! volé comme ça!* I will 'ave the law!"

A December Day in Dixie

The train was an hour and a half late. I failed to hear any complaints on that score from the few passengers who disembarked with me at Cypress Junction at 6:30 a.m. and confronted an icy blast that would better have stayed where it came from. But there was Emile Sautier's saloon just across the tracks, flaunting an alluring sign that offered to hungry wayfarers ham and eggs, fried chicken, oysters and delicious coffee at any hour.

Emile's young wife was as fat and dirty as a little pig that has slept over time in an untidy sty. Possibly she had slept under the stove; the night must have been cold. She told us Emile had come home "boozy" the night before from town. She told it before his very face and he never said a word – only went ahead pouring coal-oil on the fire that wouldn't burn. She wore over her calico dress a heavy cloth jacket with huge pearl buttons and enormous puffed sleeves, and a tattered black-white "nubia" twined about her head and shoulders as if she were contemplating a morning walk. It is impossible for me to know what her intentions were. She stood in the doorway with her little dirty, fat, ring-bedecked hands against the frame, seeming to guard the approach to an adjacent apartment in which there was a cooking stove, a bed and other articles of domestic convenience.

"Yas, he come home boozy, Emile, he don' care, him; dat's nuttin to him w'at happen'."

In his indifference to fate, the youth had lost an eye, a summer or two ago, and now he was saving no coal-oil for the lamps.

We were clamoring for coffee. Any one of us was willing to forego the fried chicken, that was huddled outside under a slanting, icy board; or the oysters, that had never got off the train; or the ham that was grunting beneath the house; or the eggs, which were possibly out where the chicken was; but we did want coffee.

Emile made us plenty of it, black as ink, since no one cared for the condensed milk which he offered with the sugar.

We could hear the chattering of a cherub in the next room where the bed and cook stove were. And when the piggish little mother went

15

in to dress it, what delicious prattle of Cadian French! what gurgling and suppressed laughter! One of my companions – there were three of us, two Natchitoches men and myself – one of them related an extraordinary experience which the infant had endured a month or two before. He had fallen into an old unused cistern a great distance from the house. In falling through the arms by some protecting limbs, and thus insecurely sustained he had called and wailed for two hours before help came.

"Yas," said his mother who had come back into the room, "'is face was black like de stove w'en we fine 'im. An' de cistern was all fill' up wid lizard' an' snake'. It was one big snake all curl' up on de udder en' de branch, lookin' at 'im de whole time." His little swarthy, rosy moon-face beamed cheerfully at us from over his mother's shoulder, and his black eyes glittered like a squirrel's. I wondered how he had lived through those two hours of suffering and terror. But the little children's world is so unreal, that no doubt it is often difficult for them to distinguish between the life of the imagination and of reality.

The earth was covered with two inches of snow, as white, as dazzling, as soft as northern snow and a hundred times more beautiful. Snow upon and beneath the moss-draped branches of the forests; snow along the bayou's edges, powdering the low, pointed, thick palmetto growths; white snow and the fields and fields of white cotton bursting from dry bolls. The Natchitoches train sped leisurely through the white, still country, and I longed for some companion to sit beside me who would feel the marvelous and strange beauty of the scene as I did. My neighbor was a gentlemen of too practical a turn.

"Oh! the cotton and the snow!" I almost screamed as the first vision of a white cotton field appeared.

"Yes, the lazy rascals; won't pick a lock of it; cotton at 4 cts, what's the use they say."

"What's the use," I agreed. How cold and inky black the negroes looked, standing in the white patches.

"Cotton's in the fields all along here and down through the bayou Natchez country."

"Oh! it isn't earthly – it's Fairyland!"

"Don't know what the planters are going to do, unless they turn half the land into pasture and start raising cattle. What you going to do with that Cane river plantation of yours?"

"God knows. I wonder if it looks like this. Do you think they've picked the cotton – Do you think one could ever forget-"

Well some kind soul should have warned us not to go into Natchitoches town. The people were all stark mad. The snow had gone to their heads.

"Keep them curtains shut tight," said the driver of the rumbling old hack. "They don't know what they about; they jus' as lief pelt you to death as not."

The horses plunged in their break neck speed; the driver swore deep under his breath; pim! pam! the missles rained against the protecting curtains; the shrieks and yells outside were demoniac, blood curdling. – There was no court that day – the judges and lawyers were rolling in the snow with the boys and girls. There was no school that day; the professors at the Normal – those from the North-states, were showing off and getting the worst of it. The nuns up on the hill and their little charges were like march hares. Barred doors were no protection if an unguarded window had been forgotten. The sanctity of home and person was a myth to be demolished with pelting, melting, showering, suffocating snow.

But the next day the sun came out and the snow all went away, except where bits of it lay here and there in protected roof angles. The magnolia leaves gleamed and seemed to smile in the sunshine. Hardy rose-vines clinging to old stuccoed pillars plumed themselves and bristled their leaves with satisfaction. And the violets peeped out to see if it was all over.

"Ah! this is a southern day," I uttered with deep gratification as I leisurely crossed the bridge afoot. A warm, gentle breeze was stirring. On the opposite side, a dear old lady was standing in her dear old doorway waiting for me.

A Harbinger

Originally appeared in *St. Louis Magazine*, 1 November 1891

Bruno did very nice work in black and white; sometimes in green and yellow and red. But he never did anything quite so clever as during that summer he spent in the hills.

The spring-time freshness had stayed, some way. And then there was the gentle Diantha, with hair the color of ripe wheat, who posed for him when he wanted. She was as beautiful as a flower, crisp with morning dew. Her violet eyes were baby-eyes – when he first came. When he went away he kissed her, and she turned red and white and trembled. As quick as thought the baby look went out of her eyes and another flashed into them.

Bruno sighed a good deal over his work that winter. The women he painted were all like mountain-flowers. The big city seemed too desolate for endurance often. He tried not to think of sweet-eyed Diantha. But there was nothing to keep him from remembering the hills; the whirr of the summer breeze through delicate-leafed maples; the bird-notes that used to break clear and sharp into the stillness when he and Diantha were together on the wooded hillside.

So when summer came again, Bruno gathered his bags, his brushes and colors and things. He whistled soft low tunes as he did so. He sang even, when he was not lost in wondering if the sunlight would fall just as it did last June, aslant the green slopes; and if – and if Diantha would quiver red and white again when he called her his sweet own Diantha, as he meant to.

Bruno had made his way through a tangle of underbrush; but before he came quite to the wood's edge, he halted: for there about the little church that gleamed white in the sun, people were gathered – old and young. He thought Diantha might be among them, and strained his eyes to see if she were. But she was not. He did see her though – when the doors of the rustic temple swung open – like a white-robed lily now.

There was a man beside her – it mattered not who; enough that it was one who had gathered this wild flower for his own, while Bruno was dreaming. Foolish Bruno! to have been only love's harbinger after all! He turned away. With hurried strides he descended the hill again, to wait by the big water-tank for a train to come along.

A Horse Story

Herminia, mounted upon a dejected looking sorrel pony, was climbing the gradual slope of a pine hill one morning in summer. She was a 'Cadian girl of the old Bayou Derbanne settlement. The pony was of the variety known indifferently as Indian, Mustang or Texan. Nothing remained of the spirited qualities of his youth. His coat in places was worn away to the hide. In other spots it grew in long tufts and clumps. To the pommel of the saddle was attached an Indian basket containing eggs packed in cotton seed; and beside, the girl carried some garden truck in a coarse bag.

From the moment of leaving her home on the bayou, Herminia had noticed a slight lump in Ti Démon's left fore foot. But to pay special attention to his peculiarities would have been to encourage him in what she considered an objectionable line of conduct. "Allons donc! You! Ti Démon! W'at's the matter with you?" she exclaimed from time to time. They had long left the bayou road and had penetrated far into the pine forest. The ascent at times was steep and the pony's feet slipped over the pine needles.

"I b'lieve you doin' on purpose!" she exclaimed vexatiously. "If I done right I would walked myse'f f'om the firs' an' lef' you behine." Ti Démon held his leg doubled at a sharp angle and seemed unable to touch it to the ground. At this, Herminia sprang from the saddle, and going forward, lifted the animal's foot to examine it.

The leg was shaggy and might have been swollen; she could not tell. But there was no sign of his having picked up a nail, a stone, or any foreign substance.

"Come 'long, Ti Démon. Courage!" and she tried to lead him by the bridle. But he could not be persuaded to move.

The girl stayed wondering what she should do. The horse could go no further; that was a self evident fact. Her own two legs were as sturdy as steel and could carry her many miles. But the question which confronted her was whether she should turn and go back home or whether she should continue on her way to Monsieur Labatier's. The planter had his summer home in the hills where there

21

were neither flies, mosquitoes, fevers, fleas nor any of the trials which often afflict the bayou dwellers in summer.

It was nearer to go to the planter's – not more than three miles. And Herminia cherished the certainty of being well received up there. Madame Labatier would pay her handsomely for the eggs and vegetables. They would invite her to dine and give her a sip of wine. She would have an opportunityof observing the toilets and manners of the young ladies – two nieces who were spending a month in the hills. But above all there would be young Mr. Prospere Labatier who perhaps would say:

"Ah! Herminia, it is too bad! Allow me to len' you my ho'se to return home," or else:

"Will you permit me the pleasure of escorting you home in my buggy?" These last considerations determined Herminia beyond further hesitancy.

With the piece of rope which she carried on such occasions she tied Ti Démon to a pine tree near the sandy road in a pleasant, shady spot.

"Now, stay there, till I come back. It's yo' own fault if you got to go hungry. You can't expec' me to tote you on my back, grosse bête!" She patted him kindly and turning her back upon him, proceeded to ascend the hill with a little springy step. She wore a calico dress of vivid red and a white sun bonnet from whose depth twinkled two black eyes, quick as a squirrel's.

Ti Démon observed her with his dull eyes and continued to hold his foot from the ground like a veritable martyr. It was still and restful in the forest and if Ti Démon had not been suffering acutely, he would have enjoyed the peaceful moment. Patches of sunlight played upon his back; a couple of red ants crawled up his hind leg; he slowly swished his long, scant tail. The mocking birds began to sing a duet in the top of a pine tree. They were young; they could sing and rejoice; they knew nothing of the tribulations attending upon old age, Ti Démon thought to himself:

"If this thing keeps up, there's no telling where it will land me."

While he understood Herminia's broken English and her mother's 'Cadian French, Ti Démon always thought in his native language, that he had imbibed in his youth in the Indian Nation.

He stood for some hours very still listening to the drowsy noises of the forest. Then a blessed relaxation began to invade the afflicted foreleg. The pain perceptibly died away, and he straightened the limb without difficulty. Ti Démon uttered a deep sigh of relief. But with the consciousness of returning comfort came the realization of his unpleasant situation. He could fancy nothing more uninteresting than to be fastened thus to a tree in the heart of the pine forest. He already began to grow hungry in anticipation of the hunger which would assail him later. He had no means of knowing what hour Herminia would return and release him from his sad predicament. It was then that Ti Démon put into practice one of his chief accomplishments. He began deliberately to unknot the rope with his old, yellow teeth. He had observed Herminia give it an extra knot and had even heard her say:

"There! if you undo that, Ti Démon, they'll have to allow you got mo' sense than Raymond's mule." The remark had offended him. He hated the constant association with Raymond's mule to which he was subjected.

He managed after persistent effort to untie the knot, and Ti Démon soon found himself free to roam whithersoever he chose. If he had been a dog he would have turned his nose uphill and followed in the footsteps of his mistress. But he was only a pony of rather low breeding and almost wholly devoid of sentiment.

Ti Démon walked leisurely down the slope, following the path by which he had come. It was a pleasing diversion to be thus permitted to roam at will. He did not linger, however, to nibble here and there after the manner of stray horses, for he knew well that the pine hill afforded little sustenance to man or beast; and he preferred to wait and whet his appetite with the luscious bits that grew below along the bayou. He appeared like a wise old philosopher plunged in thought.

By frequent stepping upon the rope dangling from his neck, it at length gave way, much to Ti Démon's satisfaction.

"Now! if I could get rid of the saddle as easily!" thought he.

It was impossible to reach the girth with his teeth; he tried that. Then Ti Démon shook himself till his coat bristled; he rubbed himself against the tree; he rolled over on his side, on his back, but the only result which he reached was to turn the saddle so that it dangled beneath him as he walked. At this he swore lustily to himself, as his master, Blanco Bill, used to swear so many years back in the Nation. He did not feel now like nibbling grass or amusing himself in any way. His one thought was to get home to his dinner of soft food and be rid of the hateful encumbrance beating against his legs.

When Ti Démon found himself standing before his home, he viewed the situation with sullen disapproval. The little house was closed and silent. The only living thing to be seen was the cat sleeping in the shade of the gallery. A line of yellow pumpkins gleamed along the boards in the sun. There was a hoe leaning up against the fence where Herminia's mother who had been hoeing the tobacco plants had left it.

"Just as I thought," grumbled Ti Démon. "I could 'a sworn to it. That woman's off gallivanting down the river again; dropped her hoe the minute Herminia's back was turned. An' them kids ought to be back from school; drat 'em! A thousand dollars to a doughnut they gone crawfishing. If I don't shake this whole shootin' match first chance I get, my name ain't Spitfire." It was thee name Blanco Bill had given him at birth and the only one he acknowledged officially.

"There's no opening gates or lifting latches or anything since they got them newfangled padlocks on," he further reflected, "if there was, I'd get inside there an' them cabbages an' cowpeas 'ld be nuts for me. Reckon I'll stroll down an' see if I c'n ketch Solistan at home." Ti Démon turned again to the road and with a deliberate stride which sent the saddle bumping and thumping, he headed for the neighboring farm up the bayou.

There was nothing startling to Solistan in seeing Ti Démon staring over his fence. He simply thought Herminia had returned from the pine hill, that the animal had got loose from the "lot" and he went forward to drive him into his own enclosure, intending to take him home later, when he should be at leisure.

But Solistan's astonishment was acute when he discovered Ti Démon's condition; covered with clay and bits of sticks and bark, Herminia's saddle hanging beneath him, and the blanket gone. It was but the work of a moment to drive the pony back in the lot; to throw a measure of corn into the trough; to saddle his own horse and start off at a mad gallop.

"Wonder what all the commotion's about," thought Ti Démon as he attempted to munch the corn from the cob. "He didn't take much trouble to pick an' choose when he gave me this mess. This here corn mus' be a hundred years old; or my teeth ain't what they used to be."

Solistan knew Ti Démon too well to believe that he had cut any capers which could have resulted in harm to Herminia. But the saddle must have turned with her; he might have stumbled and thrown her. A hundred misgivings assailed him, especially after he had been to her house and discovered the place deserted by all save the cat asleep in the shade of the gallery.

Solistan had started away just as he was, in his blue checked shirt and his boots heavy with the damp earth of the fields. He never dreamt of stopping to make a bit of toilet. He could not remember when he had in his life been a prey to such uneasiness. He had known and liked Herminia all her life; but she was always there at hand, seeming to be a natural part of the surroundings to which he was accustomed. It was only at that moment, when the menace of some dreadful and unknown fate hung over her, that he fully realized the depth and nature of his attachment for the girl.

Solistan rode far into the forest, his anxiety growing at every moment, and sick with dread of what any turn or bend in the road might reveal to him. He could not contain himself. He shouted for joy when he saw Herminia standing unharmed and motionless beneath a tall pine tree, as though she were holding a conversation and even some argument with his rugged majesty.

Her sunbonnet hung on her arm and her whole attitude was one of deep dejection. Herminia was in truth helplessly surveying the spot where she had so insecurely fastened Ti Démon, who had disappeared, leaving so much as a hair of his hide or tail to say that he had ever been there. This seeming treachery on the part of Ti

Démon marked the culmination of Herminia's mortification, and the tears were suffocating her.

Oh! it had been very fine up at the planter's! Too fine indeed. There was a large house-party congregated for the day, and little Herminia standing on the back gallery with her eggs and garden truck had been scarcely noticed.

She had been permitted to dine with them, wedged in between two stout old people; but she felt like an intruder and even perceived that the servants gave themselves the air of forgetting her. The young ladies' volubility and ease of manners made her feel small and insignificant; and their fluffy summer toilets conveyed to her only the bitter conviction of never being able to reproduce in calico such intricacy of ruffles and puffs. As for Mr. Prospere, he had only exclaimed: "Hello! Herminia!" in passing hastily along the gallery when she sat with her garden truck and eggs.

She could scarcely eat, for mortification and disappointment. She had not had an opportunity of relating the misadventure to her pony, and when, at leaving, the planter solicitously asked how she was going to get home, Herminia replied with forced dignity that she had left her horse tied a little below in the woods.

There was the wood all right, and there was Herminia, but where was the pony? That was the question which Herminia seemed to be asking of the big pine tree when Solistan rode up in such hot haste and flung himself from the saddle as if to reach out for some prize that he had pursued and captured.

"Oh! Solistan! I lef' Ti Démon fasten' yere this mornin'; he couldn' walk; an' now he's gone! Oh! Solistan! Someone mus' 'ave stole' im!"

"Ti Démon is in my lot eatin' co'n fo' all he's worth. The saddle was turned under 'im. I thought you'd got hurt." Solistan wiped his steaming , beaming hace with his bandanna; and Herminia felt at beholding him that she had never been so glad or thankful to see any one in her life. And she could not think of any one whom she would rather have seen at that moment; not even Mr. Prospere. Not even if he had come along and said:

"Allow me the pleasure of escorting you home in my buggy, Herminia!"

Solistan's was a big, broadbacked horse, and Herminia sat very comfortably behind the young man on her way back to the bayou; holding on to his suspenders when the occasion required it.

After they had reached Solistan's home and he had brought forth Ti Démon resaddled and refreshed, the following bit of conversation took place between them. Herminia was mounted, ready to start, and Solistan was still holding the animal's bridle.

"That Ti Démon of yo's is played out, Herminia. He isn't safe, I tell you. He'll play you a mean trick some these days. I been thinkin' you better use that li'l mare I traded with Raul fo' las' spring."

"Oh! Solistan! it would take too much corn to feed 'im. We got Raymond's mule to feed; an' Ti Démon eats fo' three, him-"

"Oh! shoot Ti Démon; his time's over."

"Shoot Ti Démon!" cried the girl, flushing with indignation. "You talkin' like crazy, Solistan. I would soon think o' takin' a gun an' shootin' someone passin' 'long the road."

"I'm jus' talkin'," laughed Solistan, perceiving the impression which his heartless remark had produced. "Ole Démon's good fo' a long time yet. He's plenty good to haul water or tote the children up an' down the bayou road. But don't you ever trus' yo'se'f in the woods with 'im again."

"You c'n be sho' of that, Solistan."

"An' 'bout feedin'," he went on, greatly occupied with the buckle of Ti Démon's bridle, "I could keep on feedin' the ho'se, an' if that plan don't suit you, w'at you think 'bout takin' me long with the ho'se Herminia?"

"Takin' you, Solistan!"

"W'y not? We plenty ole 'nough; you mus' be mos' eighteen, an' I'm goin; on twenty-three, me."

"I better be goin'. We c'n talk 'bout that 'nother time."

"W'en, Herminia! W'en?" implored Solistan holding on to the bridle of her pony, "tonight if I come down yonder? Say, tonight?"

"Oh Solistan, le' me go!"

"An' w'at will you tell me, Herminia?"

"We'll see 'bout that," she laughed over her shoulder as Ti Démon started away with a stiff trot.

But all the joy of life had forever left the breast of Ti Démon. Solistan's sinister remarks had made a deep and painful impression which he could not rid himself of.

When, in the autumn following, the young farmer took Herminia to be his wife, and also took Ti Démon with the benevolent intention of feeding him all the rest of his life, it was then that Ti Démon's days were given over to brooding upon the possible fate which awaited him.

Once in an unguarded moment, Ti Démon walked himself off, across Bayou Derbanne, along the Sabine and away from the haunts which had known him so long.

"If there's goin' to be any shootin'," reflected Ti Démon as he limped along, swishing his tail, "it's time fo' me to be pullin' my freight."

It was during the winter following that Solistan one evening to his wife as she bent over the fire, getting their evening meal. "W'at you think, Herminia? Raul tole me w'en he was drivin' his drove of cattle into Texas las' month, they came 'cross Ti Démon layin' dead in the Bonham road. The li'le rascal mus' a' been on his way to the Indian Nation."

"Oh! Po' Ti Démon!" exclaimed Herminia holding aloft the huge spoon with which she had been stirring the couche-couche. "He was a good an' faithful ho'se! yes!"

"That's true, Herminia," replied Solistan with philosophic resignation, "but who knows! maybe it is all fo' the best!"

A Little Country Girl

Ninette was scouring the tin milk-pail with sand and lye-soap, and bringing it to a high polish. She used for that purpose the native scrub-brush, the fibrous root of the palmetto, which she called *latanier*. The long table on which the tins were ranged, stood out in the yard under a mulberry tree. It was there that the pots and kettles were washed, the chickens, the meats and vegetables cut up and prepared for cooking.

It was all because two disagreeable old people, who had long outlived their youth, no longer believed in the circus as a means of cheering the human heart; nor could they see the use of it.

Ninette had not even mentioned the subject to them. Why should she? She might as well have said: "Grandfather and Grandmother, with your permission and a small advance, I should like, after my work is done, to make a visit to one of the distant planets this afternoon."

It was very warm and Ninette's face was red with heat and ill-humor. Her hair was black and straight and kept falling over her face. It was an untidy length; her grandmother having decided to let it grow, about six months before. She was barefooted and her calico skirt reached a little above her thick, brown ankles.

Even the negroes were all going to the circus. Suzan's daughter, who was known as Black-Gal, had lingered beside the table a moment on her way through the yard.

"You ain't gwine to de suckus?" she inquired with condescension.

"No," and bread-pan went bang on the table.

"We all's goin'. Pap an' Mammy an' all us is goin'," with a complacent air and a restful pose against the table.

"Where you all goin' to get the money, I like to know."

"Oh, Mr. Ben advance' Mammy a dollar on de crap; an' Joe, he got six bits lef' f'om las' pickin'; an' pap sole a ole no' count plow to Dennis. We all's goin'.

"Joe say he seed 'em pass yonder back Mr. Ben's lane. Dey a elephant mos' as big as dat corn-crib, walkin' long des like he somebody. An' a whole pa'cel wild critters shet up in a cage. An' all kind o' dogs an' hosses; an' de ladies rarin' an' pitchin' in red skirts all fill' up wid gole an' diamonds.

"We all's goin'. Did you ax yo' gran'ma? How come you don't ax yo' gran'pap?"

"That's my business; 'tain't none o' yo's, Black-Gal. You better be gettin' yonder home, tendin' to yo' work, I think."

"I ain't got no work, 'cep' iron out my pink flounce' dress fo' de suckus." But she took herself off with an air of lofty contempt, swinging her tattered skirts. It was after that that Ninette's tears began to drop and spatter. Resentment rose and rose within her like a leaven, causing her to ferment with wickedness and to make all manner of diabolical wishes in regard to the circus. The worst of these was that she wished it would rain.

"I hope to goodness it'll po' down rain; po' down rain; po' down rain!" She uttered the wish with the air of a young Medusa pronouncing a blighting curse.

"I like to see 'em all drippin' wet. Black-Gal with her pink flounces, all drippin' wet." She spoke these wishes in the very presence of her grandfather and grandmother, for they understood not a word of English; and she used that language to express her individual opinion on many occasions.

"What do you say, Ninette?" asked her grandmother. Ninette had brought in the last of the tin pails and was ranging them on a shelf in the kitchen.

"I said I hoped it would rain," she answered, wiping her face and fanning herself with a pie pan as though the oppressive heat had suggested the desire for a change of weather.

"You are a wicked girl," said her grandmother, turning on her, "when you know your grandfather has acres and acres of cotton ready to fall, that the rain would ruin. He's angry enough, too, with every man, woman and child leaving the fields to-day to take themselves off to the village. There ought to be a law to compel them to pick their cotton; those trifling creatures! Ah! it was different in the good old days."

Ninette possessed a sensitive soul, and she believed in miracles. For instance, if she were to go to the circus that afternoon she would consider it a miracle. Hope follows on the heels of Faith. And the white-winged goddess – which is Hope – did not leave her, but prompted her to many little surreptitious acts of preparation in the event of the miracle coming to pass.

She peeped into the clothes-press to see that her gingham dress was where she had folded and left it the Sunday before, after Mass. She inspected her shoes and got out a clean pair of stockings which she hid beneath the pillow. In the tin basin behind the house, she scrubbed her face and neck till they were red as a boiled crawfish. And her hair, which was too short to plait, she plastered and tied back with a green ribbon; it stood out in a little bristling, stiff tail.

The noon hour had hardly passed, than an unusual agitation began to be visible throughout the surrounding country. The fields were deserted. People, black and white, began passing along the road in squads and detachments. Ponies were galloping on both sides of the river, carrying two and as many as three, on their backs. Blue and green carts with rampant mules; top-buggies and no-top buggies; family carriages that groaned with age and decrepitude; heavy wagons filled with piccaninnies made a passing procession that nothing short of a circus in town could have accounted for.

Grandfather Bézeau was too angry to look at it. He retired to the hall, where he sat gloomily reading a two-weeks-old paper. He looked about ninety years old; he was in reality, not more than seventy.

Grandmother Bézeau stayed out on the gallery, apparently to cast ridicule and contempt upon the heedless and extravagant multitude; in reality, to satisfy a womanly curiosity and a natural interest in the affairs of her neighbors.

As for Ninette, she found it difficult to keep her attention fixed upon her task of shelling peas and her inward supplications that something might happen.

Something did happen. Jules Perrault, with a family load in his big farm-wagon, stopped before their gate. He handed the reins to one of the children and he, himself, got down and came up to the gallery where Ninette and her grandmother were sitting.

"What's this! what's this!"he cried out in French, "Ninette not going to the circus? not even ready to go?"

"Par example!" exclaimed the old lady, looking daggers over her spectacles. She was binding the leg of a wounded chicken that squawked and fluttered with terror.

"'*Par example*' or no '*par example*' she's going and she's going with me; and her grandfather will give her the money. Run in, little one; get ready; make haste, we shall be late." She looked appealingly at her grandmother who said nothing, being ashamed to say what she felt in the face of her neighbor, Perrault, of whom she stood a little in awe. Ninette, taking silence for consent, darted into the house to get ready.

And when she came out, wonder of wonders! There was her grandfather taking his purse from his pocket. He was drawing it out slowly and painfully, with a hideous grimace, as though it were some vital organ that he was extracting. What arguments could Mons. Perrault have used! They were surely convincing. Ninette had heard them in wordy discussion as she nervously laced her shoes; dabbed her face with flour; hooked the gingham dress; and balanced upon her head a straw "flat" whose roses looked as though they had stayed out over night in a frost. But no triumphant queen on her throne could have presented a more beaming and joyful countenance than did Ninette when she ascended and seated herself in the big wagon in the midst of Perrault family. She at once took the baby from Mme. Perrault and held it and felt supremely happy.

The more the wagon jolted and bounced, the more did it convey to her a sense of reality; and less did it seem like a dream. They passed Black-Gal and her family in the road, trudging ankle-deep in dust. Fortunately the girl was barefooted; though the pink flounces were

COLCHESTER SIXTH FORM COLLEGE LIBRARY

all there, and she carried a green parasol. Her mother was *semi-décolletée* and her father wore a heavy winter coat; while Joe had secured piece-meal, a species of cake-walk costume for the occasion. It was with a feeling of lofty disdain that Ninette passed and left the Black-Gal family in a cloud of dust.

Even after they reached the circus grounds, which were just outside the village, Ninette continued to carry the baby. She would willingly have carried three babies, had such a thing been possible. The infant took a wild and noisy interest in the merry-go-round with its hurdy-gurdy accompaniment. Oh! that she had had more money! that she might have mounted one of those flying horses and gone spinning round in a whirl of ecstasy!

There were side-shows, too. She would have liked to see the lady who weighed six hundred pounds and the gentleman who tipped the scales at fifty. She would have wanted to peep in at the curious monster, captured after a desperate struggle in the wilds of Africa. Its picture, in red and green on the flapping canvas, was surely not like anything she had ever seen of even heard of.

The lemonade was tempting: the pop-corn, the peanuts, the oranges were delights that she might only gaze upon and sigh for. Mons. Perrault took them straight to the big tent, bought the tickets and entered.

Ninette's pulses were thumping with excitement. She sniffed the air, heavy with the smell of saw-dust and animals, and it lingered in her nostrils like some delicious odor. Sure enough! There was the elephant which Black-Gal had described. A chain was about his ponderous leg and he kept reaching out his trunk for tempting morsels. The wild creatures were all there in cages, and the people walked solemnly around, looking at them; awed by the unfamiliarity of the scene.

Ninette never forgot that she had the baby in her arms. She talked to it, and it listened and looked with round, staring eyes. Later on she felt as if she were a person of distinction assisting at some royal pageant when the be-spangled Knights and Ladies in plumes and flowing robes went prancing round on their beautiful horses.

The people all sat on the circus benches and Ninette's feet hung down, because an irritable old lady objected to having them thrust into the small of her back. Mme. Perrault offered to take the baby, but Ninette clung to it. It was something to which she might communicate her excitement. She squeezed it spasmodically when her emotions became uncontrollable.

"Oh! *bébé*! I believe I'm goin' to split my sides! Oh, la! la! if gran'ma could see that, I know she'd laugh herse'f sick." It was none other than the clown who was producing this agreeable impression upon Ninette. She had only to look at his chalky face to go into contortions of mirth.

No one had noticed a gathering obscurity, and the ominous growl of thunder made every one start with disappointment or apprehension. A flash and a second clap, that was like a crash, followed. It came just as the ring-master was cracking his whip with a "hip-la! hip-la!" at the bareback rider, and the clown was standing on his head. There was a sinister roar; a terrific stroke of the wind; the center pole swayed and snapped; the great canvas swelled and beat the air with bellowing resistance.

Pandemonium reigned. In the confusion Ninette found herself down beneath piled up benches. Still clutching the baby, she proceeded to crawl out of an opening in the canvas. She stayed huddled up against the fallen tent, thinking her end had come, while the baby shrieked lustily.

The rain poured in sheets. The cries and howls of the frightened animals were like unearthly sounds. Men called and shouted; children screamed; women went into hysterics and the negroes were having fits.

Ninette got on her knees and prayed God to keep her and the baby and everyone from injury and to take them safely home. It was thus that Mons. Perrault discovered her and the baby, half covered by the fallen tent.

She did not seem to recover from the shock. Days afterward, Ninette was going about in a most unhappy frame of mind, with a wretched look upon her face. She was often covered in tears.

When her condition began to grow monotonous and depressing, her grandmother insisted upon knowing the cause of it. Then it was that she confessed her wickedness and claimed the guilt of having caused the terrible catastrophe at the circus.

It was her fault that a horse had been killed; it was her fault if an old gentleman had had a collar-bone broken and a lady an arm dislocated. She was the cause of several persons having been thrown into fits and hysterics. All her fault! She it was who had called rain down upon their heads and thus had she been punished!

It was a very delicate matter for grandmother Bézeau to pronounce upon – far too delicate. So the next day she went and explained it all to the priest and got him to come over and talk to Ninette.

The girl was at the table under the mulberry tree peeling potatoes when the priest arrived. He was a jolly little man who did not like to take things too seriously. So he advanced over the short, tufted grass, bowling low to the ground and making deep salutations with his hat.

"I am overwhelmed," he said, "at finding myself in the presence of the wonderful Magician! who has but to call upon the rain and down it comes. She whistles for the wind and – there it is! Pray, what weather will you give us this afternoon, fair Sorceress?" Then he became serious and frowning, straightened himself and rapped his stick upon the table. "What foolishness is this I hear? look at me; look at me!" for she was covering her face, "and who are you, I should like to know, that you dare think you can control the elements!"

Well, they made a great deal of fuss of Ninette and she felt ashamed.

But Mons. Perrault came over; he understood best of all. He took grandmother and grandfather aside and told them that the girl was morbid from staying so much with old people, and never associating with those of her own age. He was very impressive and convincing. He frightened them, for he hinted vaguely at terrible consequences to the child's intellect.

He must have touched their hearts, for they both consented to let her go to a birthday party over at his house the following day. Grandfather Bézeau even declared that *if it was necessary* he would contribute towards providing her with a suitable toilet for the occasion.

A Pair of Silk Stockings

Originally appeared in the magazine *Vogue* 16 September 1897.

Little Mrs. Sommers one day found herself the unexpected possessor of fifteen dollars. It seemed to her a very large amount of money, and the way in which it stuffed and bulged her worn old *porte-monnaie* gave her a feeling of importance such as she had not enjoyed for years.

The question of investment was one that occupied her greatly. For a day or two she walked about apparently in a dreamy state, but really absorbed in speculation and calculation. She did not wish to act hastily, to do anything she might afterward regret. But it was during the still hours of the night when she lay awake revolving plans in her mind that she seemed to see her way clearly toward a proper and judicious use of the money.

A dollar or two should be added to the price usually paid for Janie's shoes, which would insure their lasting an appreciable time longer than they usually did. She would buy so and so many yards of percale for new shirt waists for the boys and Janie and Mag. She had intended to make the old ones do by skillful patching. Mag should have another gown. She had seen some beautiful patterns, veritable bargains in the shop windows. And still there would be left enough for new stockings - two pairs apiece - and what darning that would save for a while! She would get caps for the boys and sailor-hats for the girls. The vision of her little brood looking fresh and dainty and new for once in their lives excited her and made her restless and wakeful with anticipation.

The neighbors sometimes talked of certain "better days" that little Mrs. Sommers had known before she had ever thought of being Mrs. Sommers. She herself indulged in no such morbid retrospection. She had no time - no second of time to devote to the past. The needs of the present absorbed her every faculty. A vision of the future like some dim, gaunt monster sometimes appalled her, but luckily to-morrow never comes.

Mrs. Sommers was one who knew the value of bargains; who could stand for hours making her way inch by inch toward the desired object that was selling below cost. She could elbow her way if need be; she had learned to clutch a piece of goods and hold it and stick to it with persistence and determination till her turn came to be served, no matter when it came.

But that day she was a little faint and tired. She had swallowed a light luncheon - no! when she came to think of it, between getting the children fed and the place righted, and preparing herself for the shopping bout, she had actually forgotten to eat any luncheon at all!

She sat herself upon a revolving stool before a counter that was comparatively deserted, trying to gather strength and courage to charge through an eager multitude that was besieging breast-works of shirting and figured lawn. An all-gone limp feeling had come over her and she rested her hand aimlessly upon the counter. She wore no gloves. By degrees she grew aware that her hand had encountered something very soothing, very pleasant to touch. She looked down to see that her hand lay upon a pile of silk stockings. A placard near by announced that they had been reduced in price from two dollars and fifty cents to one dollar and ninety-eight cents; and a young girl who stood behind the counter asked her if she wished to examine their line of silk hosiery. She smiled, just as if she had been asked to inspect a tiara of diamonds with the ultimate view of purchasing it. But she went on feeling the soft, sheeny luxurious things - with both hands now, holding them up to see them glisten, and to feel the glide serpent-like through her fingers.

Two hectic blotches came suddenly into her pale cheeks. She looked up at the girl.

"Do you think there are any eights-and-a-half among these?"

There were any number of eights-and-a-half. In fact, there were more of that size than any other. Here was a light-blue pair; there were some lavender, some all black and various shades of tan and gray. Mrs. Sommers selected a black pair and looked at them very long and closely. She pretended to be examining their texture, which the clerk assured her was excellent.

"A dollar and ninety-eight cents," she mused aloud. "Well, I'll take this pair." She handed the girl a five-dollar bill and waited for her change and for her parcel. What a very small parcel it was. It seemed lost in the depths of her shabby old shopping-bag.

Mrs. Sommers after that did not move in the direction of the bargain counter. She took the elevator, which carried her to an upper floor into the region of the ladies' waiting-rooms. Here, in a retired corner, she exchanged her cotton stockings for the new silk ones which she had just bought. She was not going through any acute mental process or reasoning with herself, nor was she striving to explain to her satisfaction the motive of her action. She was not thinking at all. She seemed for the time to be taking a rest from that laborious and fatiguing function and to have abandoned herself to some mechanical impulse that directed her actions and freed her of responsibility.

How good was the touch of the raw silk to her flesh! She felt like lying back in the cushioned chair and reveling for a while in the luxury of it. She did for a little while. Then she replaced her shoes, rolled the cotton stockings together and thrust them into her bag. After doing this she crossed straight over to the shoe department and took her seat to be fitted.

She was fastidious. The clerk could not make her out; he could not reconcile her shoes with her stockings, and she was not too easily pleased. She held back her skirts and turned her feet one way and her head another way as she glanced down at the polished, pointed-tipped boots. Her foot and ankle looked very pretty. She could not realize that they belonged to her and were a part of herself. She wanted an excellent and stylish fit, she told the young fellow who served her, and she did not mind the difference of a dollar or two more in the price so long as she got what she desired.

It was a long time since Mrs. Sommers had been fitted with gloves. On rare occasions when she had bought a pair they were always "bargains", so cheap that it would have been preposterous and unreasonable to have expected them to be fitted to the hand.

Now she rested her elbow on the cushion of the glove counter, and a pretty, pleasant young creature, delicate and deft of touch, drew a long-wristed "kid" over Mrs. Sommers' hand. She smoothed it down over the wrist and buttoned it neatly, and both lost themselves for a second or two in admiring contemplation of the little symmetrical gloved hand. But there were other places where money might be spent.

There were books and magazines piled up in the window of a stall a few paces down the street. Mrs. Sommers bought two high-priced magazines such as she had been accustomed to read in the days when she had been accustomed to other pleasant things. She carried them without wrapping. As well as she could she lifted her skirts at the crossings. Her stockings and boots and well-fitting gloves had worked marvels in her bearing - had given her a feeling of assurance, a sense of belonging to the well-dressed multitude.

She was very hungry. Another time she would have stifled the cravings for food until reaching her own home, where she would have brewed herself a cup of tea and taken a snack of anything that was available. But the impulse that was guiding her would not suffer her to entertain any such thought.

There was a restaurant at the corner. She had never entered its doors; from the outside she had sometimes caught glimpses of spotless damask and shining crystal, and soft-stepping waiters serving people of fashion.

When she entered her appearance created no surprise, no consternation, as she had half feared it might. She seated herself at a small table alone, and an attentive waiter at once approached to take her order. She did not want a profusion; she craved a nice and tasty bite - a half-dozen blue points, a plump chop with cress, a something sweet - crème-frappèe, for instance; a glass of Rhine wine, and after all a small cup of black coffee.

While waiting to be served she removed her gloves very leisurely and laid them beside her. Then she picked up a magazine and glanced through it, cutting the pages with a blunt edge of her knife. It was all very agreeable. The damask was even more spotless than it had seemed through the window, and the crystal more sparkling. There were quiet ladies and gentlemen, who did not notice her, lunching at the small tables like her own. A soft, pleasing strain of music could be heard, and a gentle breeze was blowing through the window. She tasted a bite, and she read a word or two, and she sipped the amber wine and wiggled her toes in the silk stockings. The price of it made no difference. She counted the money out to the waiter and left an extra coin on his tray, whereupon he bowed before her as before a princess of royal blood.

There was still money in her purse, and her next temptation presented itself in the shape of a matinèe poster.

It was a little later when she entered the theatre, the play had begun and the house seemed to her to be packed. But there were vacant seats here and there, and into one of them she was ushered, between brilliantly dressed women who had gone there to kill time and eat candy and display their gaudy attire. There were many others who were there solely for the play and acting. It is safe to say there was no one present who bore quite the attitude which Mrs. Sommers did to her surroundings. She gathered in the whole - stage and players and people in one wide impression, and absorbed it and enjoyed it. She laughed at the comedy and wept - she and the gaudy woman next to her wept over the tragedy. And they talked a little together over it. And the gaudy woman wiped her eyes and sniffed on a tiny square of filmy, perfumed lace and passed little Mrs. Sommers her box of candy.

The play was over, the music ceased, the crowd filed out. It was like a dream ended. People scattered in all directions. Mrs. Sommers went to the corner and waited for the cable car.

A man with keen eyes, who sat opposite to her, seemed to like the study of her small, pale face. It puzzled him to decipher what he saw there. In truth he saw nothing - unless he were wizard enough to detect a poignant wish, a powerful longing that the cable car would never stop anywhere, but go on and on with her forever.

A Point at Issue!

Originally appeared in *St. Louis Post Dispatch*, 27 Oct 1889

Married – On Tuesday, May 11, Eleanor Gail to Charles Faraday.

Nothing bearing the shape of a wedding announcement could have been less obtrusive than the foregoing hidden in a remote corner of the Plymdale *Promulgator*, clothed in the palest and smallest of type, and modestly wedged in between the big, black-lettered offer of the *Promulgator* to mail itself free of extra charge to subscribers leaving home for the summer months, and an equally somber-clad notice (doubtless astray as to place and application) that Hammersmith & Co. were carrying a large and varied assortment of marble and granite monuments!

Yet notwithstanding its sandwiched condition, that little marriage announcement seemed to Eleanor to parade the whole street.

Whichever way she turned her eyes, it glowered at her with scornful reproach.

She felt it to be an indelicate thrusting of herself upon the public notice; and at the sight she was plunged in regret at having made to the properties the concession of permitting it.

She hoped now that the period for making concessions was ended. She had endured long and patiently the trials that beset her path when she chose to diverge from the beaten walks of female Plymdaledom. Had stood stoically enough the questionable distinction of being relegated to a place amid that large and ill-assorted family of "cranks," feeling the discomfit and attending opprobrium to be far outbalanced by the satisfying consciousness of roaming the heights of free thought, and tasting the sweets of a spiritual emancipation.

The closing act of Eleanor's young ladyhood, when she chose to be married without pre-announcement, without the paraphernalia of accessories so dear to a curious public – had been in keeping with previous methods distinguishing her career. The disappointed public cheated of its entertainment, was forced to seek such compensation for the loss as was offered in reflections that while condemning her present, were unsparing of her past, and full with damning prognostic of her future.

Charles Faraday, who added to his unembellished title that of Professor of Mathematics of the Plymdale University, had found in Eleanor Gail his ideal woman.

Indeed, she rather surpassed that ideal, which had of necessity been but an adorned picture of woman as he had known her. A mild emphasizing of her merits, a soft toning down of her defects had served to offer to his fancy a prototype of that bequoted creature.

"Not too good for human nature's daily food," yet so good that he had cherished no hope of beholding such a one in the flesh. Until Eleanor had come, supplanting his ideal, and making of that fanciful creation a very simpleton by contrast. In the beginning he had found her extremely good to look at, with her combination of graceful womanly charms, unmarred by self-conscious mannerisms that was as rare as it was engaging. Talking with her, he had caught a look from her eyes into his that he recognized at once as a free masonry of intellect. And the longer he knew her, the greater grew his wonder at the beautiful revelations of her mind that unfurled itself to his, like the curling petals of some hardy blossom that opens to the inviting warmth of the sun. It was not that Eleanor knew many things. According to her own modest estimate of herself, she knew nothing. There were school girls in Plymdale who surpassed her in the amount of their positive knowledge. But she was possessed of a clear intellect: sharp in its reasoning, strong and unprejudiced in its outlook. She was that *rara avis*, a logical woman – something which Faraday had not encountered in his life before. True, he was not hoary with age. At 30 the types of women he had met with were not legion; but he felt safe in doubting that the hedges of the future would grow logical women for him, more than they had borne such prodigies in the past.

He found Eleanor ready to take broad views of life and humanity; able to grasp a question and anticipate conclusions by a quick intuition which he himself reached by the slower, consecutive steps of reason.

During the months that shaped themselves into the cycle of a year these two dwelt together in the harmony of a united purpose.

Together they went looking for the good things of life, knocking at the closed doors of philosophy; venturing into the open fields of science, she, with uncertain steps, made steady by his help.

Whithersoever he led she followed, oftentimes in her eagerness taking the lead into unfamiliar ways in which he, weighted with a lingering conservatism, had hesitated to venture.

So did they grow in their oneness of thought to belong each so absolutely to the other that the idea seemed not to have come to them that this union might be made faster by marriage. Until one day it broke upon Faraday, like a revelation from the unknown, the possibility of making her his wife.

When he spoke, eager with the new awakened impulse, she laughingly replied:

"Why not?" She had thought of it long ago.

In entering upon their new life they decided to be governed by no precedential methods. Marriage was to be a form, that while fixing legally their relation to each other, was in no wise to touch the individuality of either; that was to be preserved intact. Each was to remain a free integral of humanity, responsible to no dominating exactions of so-called marriage laws. And the element that was to make possible such a union was trust in each other's love, honor, courtesy, tempered by the reserving clause of readiness to meet the consequences of reciprocal liberty.

Faraday appreciated the need of offering to his wife advantages for culture which had been of impossible attainment during her girlhood.

Marriage, which marks too often the closing period of a woman's intellectual existence, was to be in her case the open portal through which she might seek the embellishments that her strong, graceful mentality deserved.

An urgent desire with Eleanor was to acquire a thorough speaking knowledge of the French language. They agreed that a lengthy sojourn in Paris could be the only practical and reliable means of accomplishing such an end.

Faraday's three months of vacation were to be spent by them in the idle happiness of a loitering honeymoon through the continent of Europe, then he would leave his wife in the French capital for a stay that might extend indefinitely – two, three years – as long as should be found needful, he returning to join her with the advent of each summer, to renew their love in a fresh and re-strengthened union.

And so, in May, they were married, and in September we find Eleanor established in the pension of the old couple Clairegobeau and comfortably ensconced in her pretty room that opened on to the Rue Rivoli, her heart full of sweet memories that were to cheer her coming solitude.

On the wall, looking always down at her with his quiet, kind glance, hung the portrait of her husband. Beneath it stood the fanciful little desk at which she hoped to spend many happy hours.

Books were everywhere, giving character to the graceful furnishings which their united taste had evolved from the paucity of the Clairegobeau germ, and out of the window was Paris!

Eleanor was supremely satisfied amid her new and attractive surroundings. The pang of parting from her husband seeming to lend sharp zest to a situation that offered the fulfillment of a cherished purpose.

Faraday, with the stronger man-nature, felt more keenly the discomfit of giving up a companionship that in its brief duration had been replete with the duality of accomplished delight and growing promise.

But to him also was the situation made acceptable by its involving a principle which he felt it incumbent upon him to uphold. He returned to Plymdale and to his duties at the university, and resumed his bachelor existence as quietly as though it had been interrupted but by the interval of a day.

The small public with which he had acquaintance, and which had forgotten his existence during the past few months, was fired anew with indignant astonishment at the effrontery of the situation which his singular coming back offered to their contemplation.

That two young people should presume to introduce such innovations into matrimony!

It was uncalled for!

It was improper!

It was indecent!

He must have already tired of her idiosyncrasies, since he had left her in Paris.

And in Paris, of all places, to leave a young woman alone! Why not at once in Hades?

She had been left in Paris forsooth to learn French. And since when was Mme. Belaire's French, as it had been taught to select generations of Plymdalions, considered insufficient for the practical needs of existence as related by that foreign tongue?

But Faraday's life was full with occupation and his brief moments of leisure were too precious to give to heeding the idle gossip that floated to his hearing and away again without holding his thoughts an instant.

He lived uninterruptedly a certain existence with his wife through the medium of letters. True, an inadequate substitute for her actual presence, but there was much satisfaction in this constant communion of thought between them.

They told such details of their daily lives as they thought worth the telling.

Their readings were discussed. Opinions exchanged. Newspaper cuttings sent back and forth, bearing upon questions that interested them. And what did not interest them?

Nothing was so large that they dared not look at it. Happenings, small in themselves, but big in their psychological comprehensiveness, held them with strange fascination. Her earnestness and intensity in such matters were extreme; but, happily, Faraday brought to this union humorous instincts, and an optimism that saved it from a too monotonous sombreness.

The young man had his friends in Plymdale. Certainly none that ever remotely approached the position which Eleanor held in that regard. She stood pre-eminent. She was himself.

But his nature was genial. He invited companionship from his fellow beings, who, however short that companionship might be, carried always a gratifying consciousness of having made their personalities felt.

The society in Plymdale which he most frequented was that of the Beatons.

Beaton père was a fellow professor, many years older than Faraday, but one of those men with whom time, after putting its customary stamp upon his outward being, took no further care.

The spirit of his youth had remained untouched, and formed the nucleus around which the family gathered, drawing the light of their own cheerfulness.

Mrs. Beaton was a woman whose aspirations went not further than the desire for her family's good, and her bearing announced in its every feature, the satisfaction of completed hopes.

Of the daughters, Margaret, the eldest, was looked upon as slightly erratic, owing to a timid leaning in the direction of Woman's Suffrage.

Her activity in that regard, taking the form of a desultory correspondence with members of a certain society of protest; the fashioning and donning of garments of mysterious shape, which, while stamping their wearer with the distinction of a quasi-emancipation, defeated the ultimate purpose of their construction by inflicting a personal discomfort that extended beyond the powers of long endurance. Miss Kitty Beaton, the youngest daughter, and just returned from boarding school, while clamoring for no priviledges doubtful of attainment and of remote and questionable benefit, with a Napoleonic grip, possessed herself of such rights as were at hand and exercised them in keeping the household under her capricious command.

She was at that age of blissful illusion when a girl is in love with her own youth and beauty and happiness. That age which heeds no purpose in the scope of creation further than may touch her majesty's enjoyment. Who would not smilingly endure with that charming selfishness of youth, knowing that the rough hand of experience is inevitably descending to disturb the short-lived dream?

They were all clever people, bright and interesting, and in this family circle Faraday found an acceptable relaxation from work and enforced solitude.

If they ever doubted the wisdom or expediency of his domestic relations, courtesy withheld the expression of any such doubts. Their welcome was always complete in its friendliness, and the interest which they evinced in the absent Eleanor proved that she was held in the highest esteem.

With Beaton Faraday enjoyed that pleasant intercourse which may exist between men whose ways, while not too divergent, are yet divided by an appreciable interval.

But it remained for Kitty to touch him with her girlish charms in a way, which, though not too usual with Faraday, meant so little to the man that he did not take the trouble to resent it.

Her laughter and song, the restless motions of her bubbling happiness, he watched with the casual pleasure that one follows the playful gambols of a graceful kitten.

He liked the soft shining light of her eyes. When she was near him the velvet smoothness of her pink cheeks stirred him with a feeling that could have found satisfying expression in a kiss.

It is idle to suppose that even the most exemplary men go through life with their eyes closed to woman's beauty and their senses steeled against its charm.

Faraday thought little of this feeling (and so should we if it were not outspoken).

In writing one day to his wife, with the cold-blooded impartiality of choosing a subject which he thought of neither more nor less prominence than the next, he descanted at some length upon the interesting emotions which Miss Kitty's pretty femininity aroused in him.

If he had given serious thought to the expediency of touching upon such a theme with one's wife, he still would not have been deterred. Was not Eleanor's large comprehensiveness far above the littleness of ordinary women?

Did it not enter into the scheme of their lives, to keep free from prejudices that hold their sway over the masses?

But he thought not of that, for, after all, his interest in Kitty and his interest in his university class bore about an equal reference to Eleanor and his love for her.

His letter was sent, and he gave no second thought to the matter of its contents.

The months went by for Faraday with few distinctive features to mark them outside the enduring desire for his wife's presence.

There had been a visit of sharp disturbance once when her customary letter failed him, and the tardy missive coming, carried an inexplicable coldness that dealt him a pain which, however, did not long survive a little judicious reflection and a very deluge of letters from Paris that shook him with their unusual ardor.

May had come again, and at its approach Faraday with the impatience of a hundred lovers hastened across the seas to join his Eleanor.

It was evening and Eleanor paced to and fro in her room, making the last of a series of efforts that she had been putting forth all day to fight down a misery of the heart, against which her reason was in armed rebellion. She had tried the strategy of simply ignoring its presence, but the attempt had failed utterly. During her daily walk it had embodied itself in every object that her eyes rested upon. It had enveloped her like a smoke mist, through which Paris looked more dull than the desolation of Sahara.

She had thought to displace it with work, but, like the disturbing element in the chemist's crucible, it rose again and again overspreading the surface of her labor.

Alone in her room, the hour had come when she meant to succeed by the unaided force of reason – proceeding first to make herself bodily comfortable in the folds of a majestic flowing gown, in which she looked a distressed goddess.

Her hair hung heavy and free about her shoulders, for those reasoning powers were to be spurred by a plunging of white fingers into the golden mass.

In this disheveled state Eleanor's presence seemed too large for the room and its delicate furnishings. The place fitted well an Eleanor in repose but not an Eleanor who swept the narrow confines like an incipient cyclone.

Reason did good work and stood its ground bravely, but against it were the too great odds of a woman's heart, backed by the soft prejudices of a far-reaching heredity.

She finally sank into a chair before her pretty writing desk. The golden head fell upon the outspread arms waiting to receive it, and she burst into a storm of sobs and tears. It was the signal of surrender.

It is a gratifying privilege to be permitted to ignore the reason of such unusual disturbance in a woman of Eleanor's high qualifications. The cause of that abandonment of grief will never be learned unless she chooses to disclose it herself.

When Faraday first folded his wife in his arms he saw but the Eleanor of his constant dreams. But he soon began to perceive how more beautiful she had grown; with a richness of coloring and fullness of health that Plymdale had never been able to bestow. And the object of her stay in Paris was gaining fast to accomplishment, for she had already acquired a knowledge of French that would not require much longer to perfect.

They sat together in her room discussing plans for the summer, when a timid knock at the door caused Eleanor to look up, to see the little housemaid eyeing her with the glance of a fellow conspirator and holding in her hand a card that she suffered to be but partly visible.

Eleanor hastily approached her, and reading the name upon the card thrust it into her pocket, exchanging some whispered words with the girl, among which were audible, "excuse me," "engaged," "another time." She came back to her husband looking a little flustered, to resume the conversation where it had been interrupted and he offered no inquires about her mysterious caller.

Entering the salon not many days later he found that in doing so he interrupted a conversation between his wife and a very striking looking gentleman who seemed on the point of taking his leave.

They were both disconcerted; she especially, in bowing, almost thrusting him out, had the appearance of wanting to run away; to do any thing but meet her husband's glance.

He asked with assumed indifference who her friend might be.

"Oh, no one special," with a hopeless attempt at brazenness.

He accepted the situation without protest, only indulging the reflection that Eleanor was losing something of her frankness.

But when his wife asked him on another occasion to dispense with her company for a whole afternoon, saying that she had an urgent call upon her time, he began to wonder if there might not be modifications to this marital liberty of which he was so staunch an advocate.

She left him with a hundred little endearments that she seemed to have acquired with her French.

He forced himself to the writing of a few urgent letters, but his restlessness did not permit him to do more.

It drove him to ugly thoughts, then to the means of dispelling them.

He gazed out of the window, wondered why he was remaining indoors, and followed up the reflection by seizing his hat and plunging out into the street.

The Paris boulevards of a day in early summer are calculated to dispel almost any ache but one of that nature, which was making itself incipiently felt with Faraday.

It was at that stage when it moves a man to take exception at the inadequacy of every thing that is offered to his contemplation or entertainment.

The sun was too hot.

The shop windows were vulgar; lacking artistic detail in their make-up.

How could he ever have found the Paris women attractive? They had lost their chic. Most of them were scrawny – not worth looking at.

He thought to go and stroll through the galleries of art. He knew Eleanor would wish to be with him; then he was tempted to go alone.

Finally, more tired from inward than outward restlessness, he took refuge at one of the small tables of a café, called for a "Mazarin," and, so seated for an unheeded time, let the panorama of Paris pass before his indifferent eyes.

When suddenly one of the scenes in this shifting show struck him with stunning effect.

It was the sight of his wife riding in a fiacre with her caller of a few days back, both conversing and in high spirits.

He remained for a moment enervated, then the blood came tingling back into his veins like fire, making his finger ends twitch with a desire (full worthy of any one of the "prejudiced masses") to tear the scoundrel from his seat and paint the boulevard red with his villainous blood.

A rush of wild intentions crowded into his brain.

Should he follow and demand an explanation? Leave Paris without ever looking into her face again? and more not worthy of the man.

It is right to say that his better self and better senses came quickly back to him.

That first revolt was like the unwilling protest of the flesh against the surgeon's knife before a man has steeled himself to its endurance.

Every thing came back to him from their short, common past – their dreams, their large intentions for the shaping of their lives. Here was the first test, and should he be the one to cry out, "I cannot endure it."

When he returned to the pension, Eleanor was impatiently waiting for him in the entry, radiant with gladness at his coming.

She was under a suppressed excitement that prevented her noting his disturbed appearance.

She took his listless hand and led him into the small drawing-room that adjoined their sleeping chamber.

There stood her companion of the fiacre, smiling as was she at the pleasure of introducing him to another Eleanor disposed on the wall in the best possible light to display the gorgeous radiance of her wonderful beauty and the skill of the man who had portrayed it.

The most sanguine hopes of Eleanor and her artist could not have anticipated anything like the rapture with which Faraday received this surprise.

"Monsieur l'Artiste" went away with his belief in the undemonstrativeness of the American very much shaken; and in his pocket substantial evidence of American appreciation of art.

Then the story was told how the portrait was intended as a surprise for his arrival. How there had been delay in its completion. The artist had required one more sitting, which she gave him that day, and the two had brought the picture home in the fiacre, he to give it the final advantages of a judicious light; to witness its effect upon Mons. Faraday and finally the excusable wish to be presented to the husband of the lady who had captivated his deepest admiration and esteem.

"You shall take it home with you," said Eleanor.

Both were looking at the lovely creation by the soft light of a reckless expenditure of bougie.

"Yes, dearest," he answered, with feeble elation at the prospect of returning home with that exquisite piece of inanimation.

"Have you engaged your return passage?" she asked.

She sat at his knee, arrayed in the gown that had one evening clothed such a goddess in distress.

"Oh, no. There's plenty time for that," was his answer. "Why do you ask?"

"I'm sure I don't know," and after a while:

"Charlie, I think – I mean, don't you think – I have made wonderful progress in French?"

"You've done marvels, Nellie. I find no difference between you French and Mme. Clairegobeau's, except that yours is far prettier."

"Yes?" she rejoined, with a little squeeze of the hand.

"I mayn't be right and I want you to give me your candid opinion. I believe Mme. Belaire – now that I have gone so far – don't you think – hadn't you better engage passage for two?"

His answer took the form of a pantomimic rapture of assenting gratefulness, during which each gave speechless assurance of a love that could never more take a second place.

"Nellie," he asked, looking into the face that nestled in close reach of his warm kisses, "I have often wanted to know, though you needn't tell it if it doesn't suit you," he added, laughing, "why you once failed to write to me, and then sent a letter whose coldness gave me a week's heart trouble?"

She flushed, and hesitated, but finally answered him bravely, "It was when – when you cared so much for that Kitty Beaton."

Astonishment for a moment deprived him of speech.

"But Eleanor! In the name of reason! It isn't possible!"

"I know all you would say," she replied, "I have been over the whole ground myself, over and over, but it is useless. I have found that there are certain things which a woman can't philosophize about, any more than she can about death when it touches that which is near to her."

"But you don't think-"

"Hush! don't speak of it ever again. I think nothing!" closing her eyes, and with a little shudder drawing closer to him.

As he kissed his wife with passionate fondness, Faraday thought, "I love her none the less for it, but my Nellie is only a woman, after all."

With man's usual inconsistency, he had quite forgotten the episode of the portrait.

A Reflection

Some people are born with a vital and responsive energy. It not only enables them to keep abreast of the times; it qualifies them to furnish in their own personality a good bit of the motive power to the mad pace. They are fortunate beings. They do not need to apprehend the significance of things. They do not grow weary nor miss step, nor do they fall out of rank and sink by the wayside to be left contemplating the moving procession.

Ah! that moving procession that has left me by the road-side! Its fantastic colors are more brilliant and beautiful than the sun on the undulating waters. What matter if souls and bodies are failing beneath the feet of the ever-pressing multitude! It moves with the majestic rhythm of the spheres. Its discordant clashes sweep upward in one harmonious tone that blends with the music of other worlds— to complete God's orchestra.

It is greater than the stars—that moving procession of human energy; greater than the palpitating earth and the things growing thereon. Oh! I could weep at being left by the wayside; left with the grass and the clouds and a few dumb animals. True, I feel at home in the society of these symbols of life's immutability. In the procession I should feel the crushing feet, the clashing discords, the ruthless hands and stifling breath. I could not hear the rhythm of the march.

Salve! ye dumb hearts. Let us be still and wait by the roadside.

An Idle Fellow

I am tired. At the end of these years I am very tired. I have been studying in books the languages of the living and those we call dead. Early in the fresh morning I have studied in books, and throughout the day when the sun was shining; and at night when there were stars, I have lighted my oil-lamp and studied in books. Now my brain is weary and I want rest.

I shall sit here on the door-step beside my friend Paul. He is an idle fellow with folded hands. He laughs when I upbraid him, and bids me, with a motion, hold my peace. He is listening to a thrush's song that comes from the blur of yonder apple-tree. He tells me the thrush is singing a complaint. She wants her mate that was with her last blossom-time and builded a nest with her. She will have no other mate. She will call for him till she hears the notes of her beloved-one's song coming swiftly towards her across forest and field.

Paul is a strange fellow. He gazed idly at a billowy white cloud that rolls lazily over and over along the edge of the blue sky.

He turns away from me and the words with which I would instruct him, to drink deep the scent of the clover-field and the thick perfume from the rose-hedge.

We rise from the door-step and walk together down the gentle slope of the hill; past the apple-tree, and the rose-hedge; and along the border of the field where wheat is growing. We walk down to the foot of the gentle slope where women and men and children are living.

Paul is a strange fellow. He looks into the faces of people who pass us by. He tells me that in their eyes he reads the story of their souls. He knows men and women and the little children, and why they look this way and that way. He knows the reasons that turn them to and fro and cause them to go and come. I think I shall walk a space through the world with my friend Paul. He is very wise, he knows the language of God which I have not learned.

Doctor Chevalier's Lie

Originally appeared in Vogue 5 Oct 1893

The quick report of a pistol rang through the quiet autumn night. It was no unusual sound in the unsavory quarter where Dr. Chevalier had his office. Screams commonly went with it. This time there had been none.

Midnight had already rung in the old cathedral tower.

The doctor closed the book over which he had lingered so late, and awaited the summons that was almost sure to come.

As he entered the house to which he had been called he could not but note the ghastly sameness of detail that accompanied these oft-recurring events. The same scurrying; the same groups of tawdry, frightened women bending over banisters—hysterical, some of them; morbidly curious, others; and not a few shedding womanly tears; with a dead girl stretched somewhere, as this one was.

And yet it was not the same. Certainly she was dead: there was the hole in the temple where she had sent the bullet through. Yet it was different. Other such faces had been unfamiliar to him, except so far as they bore the common stamp of death. This one was not.

Like a flash he saw it again amid other surroundings. The time was little more than a year ago. The place, a homely cabin down in Arkansas, in which he and a friend had found shelter and hospitality during a hunting expedition.

There were others beside. A little sister or two; a father and mother— coarse, and bent with toil, but proud as archangels of their handsome girl, who was too clever to stay in an Arkansas cabin, and who was going away to seek her fortune in the big city.

"The girl is dead," said Doctor Chevalier. "I knew her well, and charge myself with her remains and decent burial."

The following day he wrote a letter. One, doubtless, to carry sorrow, but no shame to the cabin down there in the forest.

It told that the girl had sickened and died. A lock of hair was sent and other trifles with it. Tender last words were even invented.

Of course it was noised about that Doctor Chevalier had cared for the remains of a woman of doubtful repute.

Shoulders were shrugged. Society thought of cutting him. Society did not, for some reason or other, so the affair blew over.

Emancipation. A Life Fable

There was once an animal born into this world, and opening his eyes upon Life, he saw above and about him confining walls, and before him were bars of iron through which came air and light from without; this animal was born in a cage.

Here he grew, and throve in strength and beauty under the care of an invisible protecting hand. Hungering, food was ever at hand. When he thirsted water was brought, and when he felt the need to rest, there was provided a bed of straw upon which to lie; and here he found it good, licking his handsome flanks, to bask in the sun beam that he thought existed but to lighten his home.

Awaking one day from his slothful rest, lo! the door of his cage stood open: accident had opened it. In the corner he crouched, wondering and fearingly. Then slowly did he approach the door, dreading the unaccustomed, and would have closed it, but for such a task his limbs were purposeless. So out the opening he thrust his head, to see the canopy of the sky grow broader, and the world waxing wider.

Back to his corner but not to rest, for the spell of the Unknown was over him, and again and again he goes to the open door, seeing each time more Light.

Then one time standing in the flood of it; a deep in-drawn breath – a bracing of strong limbs, and with a bound he was gone.

On he rushes, in his mad flight, heedless that he is wounding and tearing his sleek sides – seeing, smelling, touching of all things; even stopping to put his lips to the noxious pool, thinking it may be sweet.

Hungering there is no food but such as he must seek and ofttimes fight for; and his limbs are weighted before he reaches the water that is good to his thirsting throat.

So does he live, seeking, finding, joying and suffering. The door which accident had opened is opened still, but the cage remains forever empty!

Her Letters

I

She had given orders that she wished to remain undisturbed and moreover had locked the doors of her rooms.

The house was very still. The rain was falling steadily from a leaden sky in which there was no gleam, no rift, no promise. A generous wood fire had been lighted in the ample fireplace and it brightened and illumined the luxurious apartment to its furthermost corner.

From some remote nook of her writing desk the woman took a thick bundle of letters, bound tightly together with strong, coarse twine, and placed it upon the table in the center of the room.

For weeks she had been schooling herself for what she was about to do. There was a strong deliberation in the lines of her long, thin sensitive face; her hands, too, were long and delicate and blue-veined.

With a pair of scissors she snapped the cord binding the letters together. Thus released the ones which were top-most slid down to the table and she, with a quick movement thrust her fingers among them, scattering and turning them over till they quite covered the broad surface of the table.

Before her were envelopes of various sizes and shapes, all of them addressed in the handwriting of one man and one woman. He had sent her letters all back to her one day when, sick with dread of possibilities, she had asked to have them returned. She had meant, then, to destroy them all, his and her own. That was four years ago, and she had been feeding upon them ever since — they had sustained her, she believed, and kept her spirit from perishing utterly.

But now the days had come when the premonition of danger could no longer remain unheeded. She knew that before many months were past she would have to part from her treasure, leaving it unguarded. She shrank from inflicting the pain, the anguish which the discovery of those letters would bring to others — to one, above all, who was near to her, and whose tenderness and years of devotion had made him, in a manner, dear to her.

She calmly selected a letter at random from the pile and cast it into the roaring fire. A second one followed almost as calmly, with the third her hand began to tremble; when, in a sudden paroxysm she cast a fourth, a fifth, and a sixth into the flames in breathless succession.

Then she stopped and began to pant—for she was far from strong, and she stayed staring into the fire with pained and savage eyes. Oh, what had she done! What had she not done! With feverish apprehension she began to search among the letters before her. Which of them had she so ruthlessly, so cruelly put out of her existence? Heaven grant, not the first, that very first one written before they had learned, or dared to say to each other "I love you." No, no; there it was, safe enough. She laughed with pleasure, and held it to her lips. But what if that other most precious and most imprudent one were missing! in which every word of untempered passion had long ago eaten its way into her brain; and which stirred her still to-day, as it had done a hundred times before when she thought of it. She crushed it between her palms when she found it. She kissed it again and again. With her sharp white teeth she tore the far corner from the letter, where the name was written; she bit the torn scrap and tasted it between her lips and upon her tongue like some god-given morsel.

What unbounded thankfulness she felt at not having destroyed them all! How desolate and empty would have been her remaining days without them; with only her thoughts, illusive thoughts that she could not hold in her hands and press, as she did these, to her cheeks and her heart.

This man had changed the water in her veins to wine, whose taste had brought delirium to both of them. It was all one and past now, save for these letters that she held encircled in her arms. She stayed breathing softly and contentedly, with the hectic cheek resting upon them.

She was thinking; thinking of a way to keep them without possible ultimate injury to that other one whom they would stab more cruelly than keen knife blades.

At last she found the way. It was a way that frightened and bewildered her to think of at first, but she had reached it by deduction too sure to admit of doubt. She meant, of course, to destroy them herself before the end came. But how does the end come and when? Who may tell? She would guard against the possibility of accident by leaving them in charge of the very one who, above all, should be spared a knowledge of their contents.

She roused herself from the stupor of thought and gathered the scattered letters once more together, binding them again with the tough twine. She wrapped the compact bundle in a thick sheet of white polished paper. Then she wrote in ink upon the back of it, in large, firm characters:

"I leave this package to the care of my husband. With perfect faith in his loyalty and his love, I ask him to destroy it unopened."

It was not sealed; only a bit of string held the wrapper, which she could remove and replace at will whenever the humor came to her to pass an hour in some intoxicating dream of the days when she felt she had lived.

II

If he had come upon that bundle of letters in the first flush of his poignant sorrow there would not have been an instant's hesitancy. To destroy it promptly and without question would have seemed a welcome expression of devotion—a way of reaching her, of crying out his love to her while the world was still filled with the illusion of her presence. But months had passed since that spring day when they had found her stretched upon the floor, clutching the key of her writing desk, which she appeared to have been attempting to reach when death overtook her.

The day was much like that day a year ago when the leaves were falling and the rain pouring steadily from a leaden sky which held no gleam, no promise. He had happened accidentally upon the package in that remote nook of her desk And just as she herself had done a year ago, he carried it to the table and laid it down there, standing, staring with puzzled eyes at the message which confronted him:

"I leave this package to the care of my husband. With perfect faith in his loyalty and his love, I ask him to destroy it unopened." She had made no mistake; every line of his face—no longer young—spoke loyalty and honesty, and his eyes were as faithful as a dog's and as loving. He was a tall, powerful man, standing there in the firelight, with shoulders that stooped a little, and hair that was growing somewhat thin and gray, and a face that was distinguished, and must have been handsome when he smiled. But he was slow. "Destroy it unopened," he re-read, half aloud, "but why unopened?"

He took the package again in his hands, and turning it about and feeling it, discovered that it was composed of many letters tightly packed together.

So here were letters which she was asking him to destroy unopened. She had never seemed in her lifetime to have had a secret from him. He knew her to have been cold and passionless, but true, and watchful of his comfort and his happiness. Might he not be holding in his hands the secret of some other one, which had been confided to her and which she had promised to guard? But, no, she would have indicated the fact by some additional word or line. The secret was her own, something contained in these letters, and she wanted it to die with her.

If he could have thought of her as on some distant shadowy shore waiting for him throughout the years with outstretched hands to come and join her again, he would not have hesitated. With hopeful confidence he would have thought "in that blessed meeting-time, soul to soul, she will tell me all; till then I can wait and trust." But he could not think of her in any far-off paradise awaiting him. He felt that there was no smallest part of her anywhere in the universe, more than there had been before she was born into the world. But she had embodied herself with terrible significance in an intangible wish, uttered when life still coursed through her veins; knowing that it would reach him when the annihilation of death was between them, but uttered with all confidence in its power and potency. He was moved by the splendid daring, the magnificence of the act, which at the same time exalted him and lifted him above the head of common mortals.

What secret save one could a woman choose to have die with her? As quickly as the suggestion came to his mind, so swiftly did the man-instinct of possession creep into his blood. His fingers cramped about the package in his hands, and he sank into a chair beside the table. The agonizing suspicion that perhaps another hand shared with him her thoughts, her affections, her life, deprived him for a swift instant of honor and reason. He thrust the end of his strong thumb beneath the string which, with a single turn would have yielded—"with perfect faith in your loyalty and your love." It was not the written characters addressing themselves to the eye; it was like a voice speaking to his soul. With a tremor of anguish he bowed his head down upon the letters.

He had once seen a clairvoyant hold a letter to his forehead and purport in so doing to discover its contents. He wondered for a wild moment if such a gift, for force of wishing it, might not come to him. But he was only conscious of the smooth surface of the paper, cold against his brow, like the touch of a dead woman's hand.

A half-hour passed before he lifted his head. An unspeakable conflict had raged within him, but his loyalty and his love had conquered. His face was pale and deep-lined with suffering, but there was no more hesitancy to be seen there.

He did not for a moment think of casting the thick package into the flames to be licked by the fiery tongues, and charred and half-revealed to his eyes. That was not what she meant. He arose, and taking a heavy bronze paperweight from the table, bound it securely to the package. He walked to the window and looked out into the street below. Darkness had come, and it was still raining. He could hear the rain dashing against the window-panes, and could see it falling through the dull yellow rim of light cast by the lighted street lamp.

He prepared himself to go out, and when quite ready to leave the house thrust the weighted package into the deep pocket of his top-coat.

He did not hurry along the street as most people were doing at that hour, but walked with a long, slow, deliberate step, not seeming to mind the penetrating chill and rain driving into his face despite the shelter of his umbrella.

His dwelling was not far removed from the business section of the city; and it was not a great while before he found himself at the entrance of the bridge that spanned the river—the deep, broad, swift, black river dividing two States. He walked on and out to the very centre of the structure. The wind was blowing fiercely and keenly. The darkness where he stood was impenetrable. The thousands of lights in the city he had left seemed like all the stars of heaven massed together, sinking into some distant mysterious horizon, leaving him alone in a black, boundless universe.

He drew the package from his pocket and leaning as far as he could over the broad stone rail of the bridge, cast it from him into the river. It fell straight and swiftly from his hand. He could not follow it's descent through the darkness, nor hear its dip into the water far below. It vanished silently; seemingly into some inky unfathomable space. He felt as if he were flinging it back to her in that unknown world whither she had gone.

III

An hour or two later he sat at his table in the company of several men whom he had invited that day to dine with him. A weight had settled upon his spirit, a conviction, a certitude that there could be but one secret which a woman would choose to have die with her. This one thought was possessing him, it occupied his brain, keeping it nimble and alert with suspicion. It clutched his heart, making every breath of existence a fresh moment of pain.

The men about him were no longer the friends of yesterday; in each one he discerned a possible enemy. He attended absently to their talk. He was remembering how she had conducted herself toward this one and that one, striving to recall conversations, subtleties of facial expression that might have meant what he did not suspect at the moment, shades of meaning in words that had seemed the ordinary interchange of social amenities.

He led the conversation to the subject of women, probing these men for their opinions and experiences. There was not one but claimed some infallible power to command the affections of any woman whom his fancy might select. He had heard the empty boast before from the same group and had always met it with good-humored contempt. But to-night every flagrant, inane utterance was charged with a new meaning, revealing possibilities that, he had hitherto never taken into account.

He was glad when they were gone. He was eager to be alone, not from any desire or intention to sleep. He was impatient to regain her room, that room in which she had lived a large portion of her life, and where he had found those letters. There must surely be more of them somewhere, he thought; some forgotten scrap, some written thought or expression lying unguarded by an inviolable command.

At the hour when he usually retired for the night he sat himself down before her writing desk and began the search of drawers, slides, pigeonholes, nooks and corners. He did not leave a scrap of anything unread. Many of the letters which he found were old: some he had read before; others were new to him. But in none did he find the faintest evidence that his wife had not been the true and loyal woman he had always believed her to be. The night was nearly spent before the fruitless search ended. The brief, troubled sleep which he snatched before his hour for rising was freighted with feverish, grotesque dreams, through all of which he could hear and could see dimly the dark river rushing by, carrying away his heart, his ambitions, his life.

But it was not alone in letters that women betrayed their emotions, he thought. Often he had known them, especially when in love, to mark fugitive, sentimental passages in books of verse or prose, thus expressing and revealing their own hidden thought. Might she not have done the same?

Then began a second and far more exhausting and arduous quest than the first, turning, page by page, the volumes that crowded her room—books of fiction, poetry, philosophy. She had read them all; but nowhere, by the shadow of a sign, could he find that the author had echoed the secret of her existence—the secret which he had held in his hands and had cast into the river.

He began cautiously and gradually to question this one and that one, striving to learn by indirect ways what each had thought of her. Foremost he learned she had been unsympathetic because of her coldness of manner. One had admired her intellect; another her accomplishments; a third had thought her beautiful before disease claimed her, regretting, however, that her beauty had lacked warmth of color and expression. She was praised by some for gentleness and kindness, and by others for cleverness and tact. Oh, it was useless to try to discover anything from men! he might have known. It was women who would talk of what they knew.

They did talk, unreservedly. Most of them had loved her; those who had not had held her in respect and esteem.

IV

And yet, and yet, "there is but one secret which a woman would choose to have die with her," was the thought which continued to haunt him and deprive him of rest. Days and nights of uncertainty began slowly to unnerve him and to torture him. An assurance of the worst that he dreaded would have offered him peace most welcome, even at the price of happiness.

It seemed no longer of any moment to him that men should come and go; and fall or rise in the world; and wed and die. It did not signify if money came to him by a turn of chance or eluded him. Empty and meaningless seemed to him all devices which the world offers for man's entertainment. The food and the drink set before him had lost their flavor. He did not longer know or care if the sun shone or the clouds lowered about him. A cruel hazard had struck him there where he was weakest, shattering his whole being, leaving him with but one wish in his soul, one gnawing desire, to know the mystery which he had held in his hands and had cast into the river.

One night when there were no stars shining he wandered, restless, upon the streets. He no longer sought to know from men and women what they dared not or could not tell him. Only the river knew. He went and stood again upon the bridge where he had stood many an hour since that night when the darkness then had closed around him and engulfed his manhood.

Only the river knew. It babbled, and he listened to it, and it told him nothing, but it promised all. He could hear it promising him with caressing voice, peace and sweet repose. He could hear the sweep, the song of the water inviting him.

A moment more and he had gone to seek her, and to join her and her secret thought in the immeasurable rest.

Juanita

Originally appeared in *Moods*, July 1895

To all appearances and according to all accounts, Juanita is a character who does not reflect credit upon her family or her native town of Rock Springs. I first met her there three years ago in the little back room behind her father's store. She seemed very shy, and inclined to efface herself; a heroic feat to attempt, considering the narrow confines of the room; and a hopeless one, in view of her five-feet-ten, and more than two-hundred pounds of substantial flesh, which, on that occasion, and every subsequent one when I saw her, was clad in a soiled calico "Mother Hubbard." 1.

Her face, and particularly her mouth, had a certain fresh and sensuous beauty though I would rather not say "beauty," if I might say anything else.

I often saw Juanita that summer, simply because it was so difficult for the poor thing not to be seen. She usually sat in some obscure corner of their small garden, or behind an angle of the house, preparing vegetables for dinner or sorting her mother's flower-seed.

It was even at that day said, with some amusement, that Juanita was not so attractive to men as her appearance might indicate; that she had more than one admirer, and great hopes of marrying well if not brilliantly.

Upon my return to the "Springs" this summer, in asking news of the various persons who had interested me three years ago, Juanita came naturally to my mind, and her name to my lips. There were many ready to tell me of Juanita's career since I had seen her.

The father had died and she and the mother had had ups and downs, but still continued to keep the store. Whatever else happened, however, Juanita has never ceased to attract admirers, yound and old. They hung on her fence at all hours; they met her in the lanes; they penetrated to the store and back to the living-room. It was even talked about that a gentleman in a plaid suit had come all the way from the city by train for no other purpose than to call upon her. It is not astonishing, in the face of these persistent attentions, that speculation grew rife in Rock Springs as to whom and what Juanita would marry in the end.

For a while she was said to be engaged to a wealthy South Missouri farmer, though no one could guess when or where she had met him. Then it was learned that the man of her choice was a Texas millionaire who possessed a hundred white horses, one of which spirited animals Juanita began to drive about that time.

But in the midst of speculation and counter speculation on the subject of Juanita and her lovers, there suddenly appeared upon the scene a one-legged man; a very poor and shabby, and decidedly one-legged man. He first became known to the public through Juanita's soliciting subscriptions towards buying the unhappy individual cork-leg.

But in the midst of the speculation and counter speculation on the subject of Juanita and her lovers, there suddenly appeared upon the scene a one-legged man; a very poor and shabby and decidedly one-legged man. He first became know to the public through Juanita's soliciting subscriptions towards buying the unhappy individual a cork-leg.

Her interest in the one-legged man continued to show itself in various ways, not always apparent to a curious public; as was proven one morning when Juanita became the mother of a baby, whose father, she announced, was her husband, the one-legged man. The story of a wandering preacher was told; a secret marriage in the state of Illinois; and a lost certificate.

However that may be, Juanita has turned her broad back upon the whole race of masculine bipeds, and lavishes the wealth of her undivided affections upon the one-legged man.

I caught a glimpse of the curious couple when I was in the village. Juanita had mounted her husband upon a dejected looking pony which she herself was apparently leading by the bridle, and they were moving up the lane towards the woods, whither, I am told, they often wander in this manner. The picture they presented was a singular one; she with a man's straw hat shading her inflamed moon-face, and the breeze bellying her soiled "Mother Hubbard" into monstrous proportions. He puny, helpless, but apparently content with his fate which had not even vouchsafed him the coveted cork-leg.

They go off thus to the woods together where they may love each other away from all prying eyes save those of the birds and the squirrels. But what do the squirrels care!

For my part I never expected Juanita to be more respectable than a squirrel; and I don't see how any one else could have expected it.

---

1. A loose, shapeless dress

Lilacs

Mme. Adrienne Farival never announced her coming; but the good nuns knew very well when to look for her. When the scent of the lilac blossoms began to permeate the air, Sister Agathe would turn many times during the day to the window; upon her face the happy, beatific expression with which pure and simple souls watch for the coming of those they love.

But it was not Sister Agathe; it was Sister Marceline who first espied her crossing the beautiful lawn that sloped up to the convent. Her arms were filled with great bunches of lilacs which she had gathered along her path. She was clad all in brown; like one of the birds that come with the spring, the nuns used to say. Her figure was rounded and graceful, and she walked with a happy, buoyant step. The cabriolet which had conveyed her to the convent moved slowly up the gravel drive that led to the imposing entrance. Beside the driver was her modest little, black trunk, with her name and address printed in white letters upon it: "Mme. A. Farival, Paris." It was the crunching of the gravel which had attracted Sister Marceline's attention. And then the commotion began.

White-capped heads appeared suddenly at the windows; she waved her parasol and her bunch of lilacs at them. Sister Marceline and Sister Marie Anne appeared, fluttered and expectant at the doorway. But Sister Agathe, more daring and impulsive than all, descended the steps and flew across the grass to meet her. What embraces, in which the lilacs were crushed between them! What ardent kisses! What pink flushes of happiness mounting the cheeks of the two women!

Once within the convent Adrienne's soft brown eyes moistened with tenderness as they dwelt caressingly upon the familiar objects about her, and noted the most trifling details. The white, bare boards of the floor had lost nothing of their luster. The stiff, wooden chairs, standing in rows against the walls of hall and parlor, seemed to have taken on an extra polish since she had seen them, last lilac time. And there was a new picture of the Sacré-Coeur hanging over the hall table. What had they done with Ste. Catherine de Sienne, who had occupied that position of honor for so many years? In the chapel—it was no use trying to deceive her—she saw at a glance that St. Joseph's mantle had been embellished with a new coat of blue, and the aureole about his head freshly gilded. And the Blessed Virgin there neglected! Still wearing her garb of last spring, which looked almost dingy by contrast. It was not just-such partiality! The Holy Mother had reason to be jealous and to complain.

But Adrienne did not delay to pay her respects to the Mother Superior, whose dignity would not permit her to so much as step outside the door of her private apartments to welcome this old pupil. Indeed, she was dignity in person; large, uncompromising, unbending She kissed Adrienne without warmth, and discussed conventional themes learnedly and prosaically during the quarter of an hour which the young woman remained in her company.

It was then that Adrienne's latest gift was brought in for inspection. For Adrienne always brought a handsome present for the chapel in her little black trunk. Last year it was a necklace of gems for the Blessed Virgin, which the Good Mother was only permitted to wear on extra occasions, such as great feast days of obligation. The year before it had been a precious crucifix—an ivory figure of Christ suspended from an ebony cross, whose extremities were tipped with wrought silver. This time it was a linen embroidered altar cloth of such rare and delicate workmanship that the Mother Superior, who knew the value of such things, chided Adrienne for the extravagance.

"But, dear Mother, you know it is the greatest pleasure I have in life—to be with you all once a year, and to bring some such trifling token of my regard."

The Mother Superior dismissed her with the rejoinder: "Make yourself at home, my child. Sister Thérèse will see to your wants. You will occupy Sister Marceline's bed in the end room, over the chapel. You will share the room with Sister Agathe."

There was always one of the nuns detailed to keep Adrienne company during her fortnight's stay at the convent. This had become almost a fixed regulation. It was only during the hours of recreation that she found herself with them all together. Those were hours of much harmless merry-making under the trees or in the nuns' refectory.

This time it was Sister Agathe who waited for her outside of the Mother Superior's door. She was taller and slenderer than Adrienne, and perhaps ten years older. Her fair blond face flushed and paled with every passing emotion that visited her soul. The two women linked arms and went together out into the open air.

There was so much which Sister Agathe felt that Adrienne must see. To begin with, the enlarged poultry yard, with its dozens upon dozens of new inmates. It took now all the time of one of the lay sisters to attend to them. There had been no change made in the vegetable garden, but—yes there had; Adrienne's quick eye at once detected it. Last year old Philippe had planted his cabbages in a large square to the right. This year they were set out in an oblong bed to the left. How it made Sister Agathe laugh to think Adrienne should have noticed such a trifle! And old Philippe, who was nailing a broken trellis not far off, was called forward to be told about it.

He never failed to tell Adrienne how well she looked, and how she was growing younger each year. And it was his delight to recall certain of her youthful and mischievous escapades. Never would he forget that day she disappeared; and the whole convent in a hubbub about it! And how at last it was he who discovered her perched among the tallest branches of the highest tree on the grounds, where she had climbed to see if she could get a glimpse of Paris! And her punishment afterwards!—half of the Gospel of Palm Sunday to learn by heart!

We may laugh over it, my good Philippe, but we must remember that Madame is older and wiser now."

"I know well, Sister Agathe, that one ceases to commit follies after the first days of youth." And Adrienne seemed greatly impressed by the wisdom of Sister Agathe and old Philippe, the convent gardener.

A little later when they sat upon a rustic bench which overlooked the smiling landscape about them, Adrienne was saying to Sister Agathe, who held her hand and stroked it fondly:

"Do you remember my first visit, four years ago, Sister Agathe? and what a surprise it was to you all!"

"As if I could forget it, dear child!"

"And I! Always shall I remember that morning as I walked along the boulevard with a heaviness of heart—oh, a heaviness which I hate to recall. Suddenly there was wafted to me the sweet odor of lilac blossoms. A young girl had passed me by, carrying a great bunch of them. Did you ever know, Sister Agathe, that there is nothing which so keenly revives a memory as a perfume—an odor?"

"I believe you are right, Adrienne. For now that you speak of it, I can feel how the odor of fresh bread—when Sister Jeanne bakes—always makes me think of the great kitchen of ma tante de Sierge, and crippled Julie, who sat always knitting at the sunny window. And I never smell the sweet scented honeysuckle without living again through the blessed day of my first communion."

"Well, that is how it was with me, Sister Agathe, when the scent of the lilacs at once changed the whole current of my thoughts and my despondency. The boulevard, its noises, its passing throng., vanished from before my senses as completely as if they had been spirited away. I was standing here with my feet sunk in the green sward as they are now. I could see the sunlight glancing from that old white stone wall, could hear the notes of birds, just as we hear them now, and the humming of insects in the air. And through all I could see and could smell the lilac blossoms, nodding invitingly to me from their thick-leaved branches. It seems to me they are richer than ever this year, Sister Agathe. And do you know, I became like an enragée; nothing could have kept me back. I do not remember now where I was going; but I turned and retraced my steps homeward in a perfect fever of agitation: 'Sophie! My little trunk—quick—the black one! A mere handful of clothes! I am going away. Don't ask me any questions. I shall be back in a fortnight.' And every year since then it is the same. At the very first whiff of a lilac blossom, I am gone! There is no holding me back."

"And how I wait for you, and watch those lilac bushes, Adrienne! If you should once fail to come, it would be like the spring coming without the sunshine or the song of birds.

"But do you know, dear child, I have sometimes feared that in moments of despondency such as you have just described, I fear that you do not turn as you might to our Blessed Mother in heaven, who is ever ready to comfort and solace an afflicted heart with the precious balm of her sympathy and love."

"Perhaps I do not, dear Sister Agathe. But you cannot picture the annoyances which I am constantly submitted to. That Sophie alone, with her detestable ways! I assure you she of herself is enough to drive me to St. Lazare."

"Indeed, I do understand that the trials of one living in the world must be very great, Adrienne; particularly for you, my poor child, who have to bear them alone, since Almighty God was pleased to call to himself your dear husband. But on the other hand, to live one's life along the lines which our dear Lord traces for each one of us, must bring with it resignation and even a certain comfort. You have your household duties, Adrienne, and your music, to which, you say, you continue to devote yourself. And then, there are always good works—the poor—who are always with us—to be relieved; the afflicted to be comforted."

"But, Sister Agathe! Will you listen! Is it not La Rose that I hear moving down there at the edge of the pasture? I fancy she is reproaching me with being an ingrate, not to have pressed a kiss yet on that white forehead of hers. Come, let us go."

The two women arose and walked again, hand in hand this time, over the tufted grass down the gentle decline where it sloped toward the broad, flat meadow, and the limpid stream that flowed cool and fresh from the woods. Sister Agathe walked with her composed, nunlike tread; Adrienne with a balancing motion, a bounding step, as though the earth responded to her light footfall with some subtle impulse all its own.

They lingered long upon the foot-bridge that spanned the narrow stream which divided the convent grounds from the meadow beyond. It was to Adrienne indescribably sweet to rest there in soft, low converse with this gentle-faced nun, watching the approach of evening. The gurgle of the running water beneath them; the lowing of cattle approaching in the distance, were the only sounds that broke upon the stillness, until the clear tones of the angelus bell pealed out from the convent tower. At the sound both women instinctively sank to their knees, signing themselves with the sign of the cross. And Sister Agathe repeated the customary invocation, Adrienne responding in musical tones:

"The Angel of the Lord declared unto Mary, And she conceived by the Holy Ghost—"

and so forth, to the end of the brief prayer, after which they arose and retraced their steps toward the convent.

It was with subtle and naive pleasure that Adrienne prepared herself that night for bed. The room which she shared with Sister Agathe was immaculately white. The walls were a dead white, relieved only by one florid print depicting Jacob's dream at the foot of the ladder, upon which angels mounted and. descended. The bare floors, a soft yellow-white, with two little patches of gray carpet beside each spotless bed. At the head of the white-draped beds were two bénitiers containing holy water absorbed in sponges.

Sister Agathe disrobed noiselessly behind her curtains and glided into bed without having revealed, in the faint candlelight, as much as a shadow of herself. Adrienne pattered about the room, shook and folded her garments with great care, placing them on the back of a chair as she had been taught to do when a child at the convent. It secretly pleased Sister Agathe to feel that her dear Adrienne clung to the habits acquired in her youth.

But Adrienne could not sleep. She did not greatly desire to do so. These hours seemed too precious to be cast into the oblivion of slumber.

"Are you not asleep, Adrienne?"

"No, Sister Agathe. You know it is always so the first night. The excitement of my arrival—I don't know what—keeps me awake."

"Say your 'Hail, Mary,' dear child, over and over." "I have done so, Sister Agathe; it does not help."

"Then lie quite still on your side and think of nothing but your own respiration. I have heard that such inducement to sleep seldom fails."

"I will try. Good night, Sister Agathe.

"Good night, dear child. May the Holy Virgin guard you."

An hour later Adrienne was still lying with wide, wakeful eyes, listening to the regular breathing of Sister Agathe. The trailing of the passing wind through the treetops, the ceaseless babble of the rivulet were some of the sounds that came to her faintly through the night.

The days of the fortnight which followed were in character much like the first peaceful, uneventful day of her arrival, with the exception only that she devoutly heard mass every morning at an early hour in the convent chapel, and on Sundays sang in the choir in her agreeable, cultivated voice, which was heard with delight and the warmest appreciation.

When the day of her departure came, Sister Agathe was not satisfied to say good-bye at the portal as the others did. She walked down the drive beside the creeping old cabriolet, chattering her pleasant last words. And then she stood-it was as far as she might go—at the edge of the road, waving good-bye in response to the fluttering of Adrienne's handkerchief. Four hours later Sister Agathe, who was instructing a class of little girls for their first communion, looked up at the classroom clock and murmured: "Adrienne is at home now.""

Yes, Adrienne was at home. Paris had engulfed her.

At the very hour when Sister Agathe looked up at the clock, Adrienne, clad in a charming negligee, was reclining indolently in the depths of a luxurious armchair. The bright room was in its accustomed state of picturesque disorder. Musical scores were scattered upon the open piano. Thrown carelessly over the backs of chairs were puzzling and astonishing-looking garments.

In a large gilded cage near the window perched a clumsy green parrot. He blinked stupidly at a young girl in street dress who was exerting herself to make him talk.

In the center of the room stood Sophie, that thorn in her mistress s side. With hands plunged in the deep pockets of her apron, her white starched cap quivering with each emphatic motion of her grizzled head, she was holding forth, to the evident ennui of the two young women. She was saying:

"Heaven knows I have stood enough in the six years I have been with Mademoiselle; but never such indignities as I have had to endure in the past two weeks at the hands of that man who calls himself a manager! The very first day—and I, good enough to notify him at once of Mademoiselle's flight—he arrives like a lion; I tell you, like a lion. He insists upon knowing Mademoiselle's whereabouts. How can I tell him any more than the statue out there in the square? He calls me a liar! Me, me—a liar! He declares he is ruined. The public will not stand La Petite Gilberta in the role which Mademoiselle has made so famous-La Petite Gilberta, who dances like a jointed wooden figure and sings like a traînée of a café chantant. If I were to tell La Gilberta that, as I easily might, I guarantee it would not be well for the few straggling hairs which he has left on that miserable head of his!

"What could he do? He was obliged to inform the public that Mademoiselle was ill; and then began my real torment! Answering this one and that one with their cards, their flowers, their dainties in covered dishes! which, I must admit, saved Florine and me much cooking. And all the while having to tell them that the physician had advised for Mademoiselle a rest of two weeks at some watering-place, the name of which I had forgotten!"

Adrienne had been contemplating old Sophie with quizzical, half-closed eyes, and pelting her with hot-house roses which lay in her lap, and which she nipped off short from their graceful stems for that purpose. Each rose struck Sophie full in the face; but they did not disconcert her or once stem the torrent of her talk.

"Oh, Adrienne!" entreated the young girl at the parrot's cage. "Make her hush; please do something. How can you ever expect Zozo to talk? A dozen times he has been on the point of saying something! I tell you, she stupefies him with her chatter."

"My good Sophie," remarked Adrienne, not changing her attitude, "you see the roses are all used up. But I assure you, anything at hand goes," carelessly picking up a book from the table beside her. "What is this? Mons. Zola! Now I warn you,, Sophie, the weightiness, the heaviness of Mons. Zola are such that they cannot fail to prostrate you; thankful you may be if they leave you with energy to regain your feet."

"Mademoiselle's pleasantries are all very well; but if I am to be shown the door for it—if I am to be crippled for it—I shall say that I think Mademoiselle is a woman without conscience and without heart. To torture a man as she does! A man? No, an angel

"Each day he has come with sad visage and drooping mien. 'No news, Sophie?'

"'None, Monsieur Henri.' 'Have you no idea where she has gone?' 'Not any more than the statue in the square, Monsieur. 'Is it perhaps possible that she may not return at all?' with his face blanching like that curtian.

"I assure him you will be back at the end of the fortnight. I entreat him to have patience. He drags himself, desole, about the room, picking up Mademoiselle's fan, her gloves, her music, and turning them over and over in his hands. Mademoiselle's slipper, which she took off to throw at me in the impatience of her departure, and which I purposely left lying where it fell on the chiffonier—he kissed it—I saw him do it—and thrust it into his pocket, thinking himself unobserved.

"The same song each day. I beg him to eat a little good soup which I have prepared. 'I cannot eat, my dear Sophie.' The other night he came and stood long gazing out of the window at the stars. When he turned he was wiping his eyes; they were red. He said he had been riding in the dust, Which had inflamed them. But I knew better; he had been crying.

"Ma foi! in his place I would snap my finger at such cruelty. I would go out and amuse myself. What is the use of being young!"

Adrienne arose with a laugh. She went and seizing old Sophie by the shoulders shook her till the white cap wobbled on her head.

"What is the use of all this litany, my good Sophie? Year after year the same! Have you forgotten that I have come a long, dusty journey by rail, and that lam perishing of hunger and thirst? Bring us a bottle of Château Yquem and a biscuit and my box of cigarettes." Sophie had freed herself, and was retreating toward the door. "'And, Sophie! If Monsieur Henri is still waiting, tell him to come up."

It was precisely a year later. The spring had come again, and Paris was intoxicated.

Old Sophie sat in her kitchen discoursing to a neighbor who had come in to borrow some trifling kitchen utensil from the old bonne.

"You know, Rosalie, I begin to believe it is an attack of lunacy which seizes her once a year. I wouldn't say it to everyone, but with you I know it will go no further. She ought to be treated for it; a physician should be consulted; it is not well to neglect such things and let them run on.

"It came this morning like a thunder clap. As I am sitting here, there had been no thought or mention of a journey. The baker had come into the kitchen—you know what a gallant he is—with always a girl in his eye. He laid the bread down upon the table and beside it a bunch of lilacs. I didn't know they had bloomed yet. 'For Mam'selle Florine, with my regards,' he said with his foolish simper.

"Now, you know I was not going to call Florine from her work in order to present her the baker's flowers. All the same, it would not do to let them wither. I went with them in my hand into the dining room to get a majolica pitcher which I had put away in the closet there, on an upper shelf, because the handle was broken. Mademooiselle, who rises, early, had just come from her bath, and was crossing the hall that opens into the dining room. just as she was, in her white peignoir, she thrust her head into the dining room, snuffling the air and exclaiming, 'What do I smell?'

"She espied the flowers in my hand and pounced upon them like a cat upon a mouse. She held them up to her, burying her face in them for the longest time, only uttering a long 'Ah!'

"'Sophie, I am going away—Get out the little black trunk; a few of the plainest garments I have; my brown dress that I have not yet worn.'

"'But, Mademoiselle,' I protested, 'you forget that you have ordered a breakfast of a hundred francs for tomorrow.'

"'Shut up!' she cried, stamping her foot.

"'You forget how the manager will rave,' I persisted, 'and vilify me. And you will go like that without a word of adieu to Monsieur Paul, who is an angel if ever one trod the earth.'

"I tell you, Rosalie, her eyes flamed.

"'Do as I tell you this instant,' she exclaimed, 'or I will strangle you—with your Monsieur Paul and your manager and your hundred francs!'"

"Yes," affirmed Rosalie, "it is insanity. I had a cousin seized in the same way one morning, when she smelled calf's liver frying with onions. Before night it took two men to hold her."

"I could well see it was insanity, my dear Rosalie, and I uttered not another word as I feard for my life. I simply obeyed her every command in silence. And now—whiff, she is gone! God knows where. But between us, Rosalie—I wouldn't say it to Florine—but I believe it is for no good. I, in Monsieur Paul's place, should have her watched. I would put a detective upon her track.

"Now I am going to close up; barricade the entire establishment. Monsieur Paul, the manager, visitors, all—all may ring and knock and shout themselves hoarse. I am tired of it all. To be vilified and called a liar—at my age, Rosaile!"

Adrienne left her trunk at the small railway station, as the old cabriolet was not at the moment available; and she gladly walked the mile or two of pleasant roadway which led to the convent. How infinitely calm, peaceful, penetrating was the charm of the verdant, undulating country spreading out on all sides of her! She walked along the clear smooth road, twirling her parasol; humming a gay tune; nipping here and there a bud or a waxlike leaf from the hedges along the way; and all the while drinking deep draughts of complacency and content.

She stopped, as she had always done, to pluck lilacs in her path.

As she approached the convent she fancied that a whitecapped face had glanced fleetingly from a window; but she must have been mistaken. Evidently she had not been seen, and this time would take them by surprise. She smiled to think how Sister Agathe would utter a little joyous cry of amazement, and in fancy she already felt the warmth and tenderness of the nun's embrace. And how Sister Marceline and the others would laugh, and make game of her puffed sleeves! For puffed sleeves had come into fashion since last year, and the vagaries of fashion always afforded infinite merriment to the nuns. No, they surely had not seen her.

She ascended lightly the stone steps and rang the bell. She could hear the sharp metallic sound reverberate through the halls. Before its last note had died away the door was opened very slightly, very cautiously by a lay sister who stood there with downcast eyes and flaming cheeks. Through the narrow opening she thrust forward toward Adrienne a package and a letter, saying, in confused tones: "By order of our Mother Superior." After which she closed the door hastily and turned the heavy key in the great lock.

Adrienne remained stunned. She could not gather her faculties to grasp the meaning of this singular reception. The lilacs fell from her arms to the stone portico on which she was standing. She turned the note and the parcel stupidly over in her hands, instinctively dreading what their contents might disclose.

The outlines of the crucifix were plainly to be felt through the wrapper of the bundle, and she guessed, without having courage to assure herself, that the jeweled necklace and the altar cloth accompanied it.

Leaning against the heavy oaken door for support, Adrienne opened the letter. She did not seem to read the few bitter reproachful lines word by word—the lines that banished her forever from this haven of peace, where her soul was wont to come and refresh itself. They imprinted themselves as a whole upon her brain, in all their seeming cruelty—she did not dare to say injustice.

There was no anger in her heart; that would doubtless possess her later, when her nimble intelligence would begin to seek out the origin of this treacherous turn. Now, there was only room for tears. She leaned her forehead against the heavy oaken panel of the door and wept with the abandonment of a little child.

She descended the steps with a nerveless and dragging tread. Once as she was walking away, she turned to look back at the imposing facade of the convent, hoping to see a familiar face, or a hand, even, giving a faint token that she was still cherished by some one faithful heart. But she saw only the polished windows looking down at her like so many cold and glittering and reproachful eyes.

In the little white room above the chapel, a woman knelt beside the bed on which Adrienne had slept. Her face was pressed deep in the pillow in her efforts to smother the sobs that convulsed her frame. It was Sister Agathe.

After a short while, a lay sister came out of the door with a broom, and swept away the lilac blossoms which Adrienne had let fall upon the portico.

Miss McEnders

I

When Miss Georgie McEnders had finished an elaborately simple toilet of gray and black, she divested herself completely of rings, bangles, brooches – everything to suggest that she stood in friendly relations with fortune. For Georgie was going to read a paper upon "The Dignity of Labor" before the Woman's Reform Club; and if she was blessed with the abundance of wealth, she possessed a no less amount of good taste.

Before entering the neat Victoria that stood at her father's too-sumptuous door – and that was her special property – she turned to give certain directions to the coachman. First upon the list from which she read was inscribed: "Look up Mademoiselle Salambre."

"James," said Georgie, flushing a pretty pink, as she always did with the slightest effort of speech, "we want to look up a person named Mademoiselle Salambre, in the southern part of town, on Arsenal street," indicating a certain number and locality. Then she seated herself in the carriage, and as it drove away proceeded to study her engagement list further and to knit her pretty brows in deep and complex thought.

"Two o'clock – look up M. Salambre," said the list. "Three-thirty – read paper before Woman's Ref. Club. Four-thirty – "and here followed cabalistic abbreviations which meant: "Join committee of ladies to investigate moral condition of St. Louis factory-girls. Six o'clock – dine with papa. Eight o'clock – hear Henry George's lecture on Single Tax."

So far, Mademoiselle Salambre was only a name to Georgie McEnders, one of several submitted to her at her own request by her furnishers, Push and Prodem, an enterprising firm charged with the construction of Miss McEnders' very elaborate trosseau. Georgie liked to know the people who worked for her, as far as she could.

She was a charming young woman of twenty-five, though almost too white-souled for a creature of flesh and blood. She possessed ample wealth and time to squander, and a burning desire to do good – to elevate the human race, and start the world over again on a comfortable footing for everybody.

When Georgie had pushed open the very high gate of a very small yard she stood confronting a robust German woman who, with dress tucked carefully between her knees, was in the act of noisily "redding" the bricks.

"Does M'selle Salambre live here?" Georgie's tall, slim figure was very erect. Her face suggested a sweet peach blossom, and she held a severely simple lorgnon up to her short-sighted blue eyes.

"Ya! Ya! Aber oop stairs!" cried the woman brusquely and impatiently. But Georgie did not mind. She was used to greetings that lacked the ring of cordiality.

When she had ascended the stairs that led to an upper porch she knocked at the first door that presented itself, and was told to enter by Mlle. Salambre herself.

The woman sat at an opposite window, bending over a bundle of misty white goods that lay in a fluffy heap in her lap. She was not young. She might have been thirty, or she might have been forty. There were lines about her round, piquante face that denoted close acquaintance with struggles, hardships and all manner of unkind experiences.

Georgie had heard a whisper here and there touching the private character of Mlle. Salambre which had determined her to go in person and make the acquaintance of the woman and her surroundings; which latter were poor and simple enough, and not too neat. There was a little child at play upon the floor.

Mlle. Salambre had not expected so unlooked-for an apparition as Miss McEnders, and seeing the girl standing there in the door she removed the eye-glasses that had assisted her in the delicate work, and stood up also.

"Mlle. Salambre, I suppose?" said Georgie, with a courteous inclination.

"Ah! Mees McEndairs! What an agree'ble surprise! Will you be so kind to take a chair." Mademoiselle had lived many years in the city, in various capacities, which brought her in touch with the fashionable set. There were few people in polite society whom Mademoiselle did not know – by sight, at least; and their private histories were as familiar to her as her own.

"You 'ave come to see your the work?" the woman went on with a smile that quite brightened her face. "It is a pleasure to handle such fine, such delicate quality of goods, Mees," and she went and laid several pieces of her handiwork upon the table beside Georgie, at the same time indicating such details as she hoped would call forth her visitor's approval.

There was something about the woman and her surroundings, and the atmosphere of the place, that affected the girl unpleasantly. She shrank instinctively, drawing her invisible mantle of chastity closely about her. Mademoiselle saw that her visitor's attention was divided between the lingerie and the child upon the floor, who was engaged in battering a doll's unyielding head against the unyielding floor.

"The child of my neighbor down-stairs," said Mademoiselle, with a wave of the hand which expressed volumes of unutterable ennui. But at that instant the little one, with instinctive mistrust, and in seeming defiance of the repudiation, climbed to her feet and went rolling and toddling towards her mother, clasping the woman about the knees, and calling her by the endearing title which was her own small right.

A spasm of annoyance passed over Mademoiselle's face, but still she called the child "*Chene,*" as she grasped its arm to keep it from falling. Miss McEnders turned every shade of carmine.

"Why did you tell me an untruth?" she asked, looking indignantly into the woman's lowered face. "Why do you call yourself 'Mademoiselle' if this child is yours?"

"For the reason that it is more easy to obtain employment. For reasons that you would not understand," she continued, with a shrug of the shoulders that expressed some defiance and a sudden disregard for consequences. "Life is not all *couleur de rose*, Mees McEndairs; you do not know what life is, you!" And drawing a handkerchief from an apron pocket she mopped an imaginary tear from the corner of her eye, and blew her nose till it glowed again.

Georgie could hardly recall the words or actions with which she quitted Mademoiselle's presence. As much as she wanted to, it had been impossible to stand and read the woman a moral lecture. She had simply thrown what disapproval she could into her hasty leave-taking, and that was all for the moment. But as she drove away, a more practical form of rebuke suggested itself to her not too nimble intelligence – one that she promised herself to act upon as soon as her home was reached.

When she was alone in her room, during an interval between her many engagements, she then attended to the affair of Mlle. Salambre.

Georgie believed in discipline. She hated unrighteousness. When it pleased God to place the lash in her hand she did not hesitate to apply it. Here was this Mlle. Salambre living in her sin. Not as one who is young and blinded by the glamour of pleasure, but with cool and deliberate intention. Since she chose to transgress, she ought to suffer, and be made to feel that her ways were iniquitous and invited rebuke. It lay in Georgie's power to mete out a small dose of that chastisement which the woman deserved, and she was glad that the opportunity was hers.

She seated herself forthwith at her writing table, and penned the following note to her furnishers:

"MESSERS. PUSH & PRODEM.

"*Gentlemen* – Please withdraw from Mademoiselle Salambre all work of mine, and return same to me at once – finished or unfinished.
Yours truly,

GEORGIE MCENDERS."

II

On the second day following this summary proceeding, Georgie sat at her writing-table, looking prettier and pinker than ever, in a luxurious and soft-toned robe de chambre that suited her own delicate coloring, and fitted the pale amber tints of her room decorations.

There were books, pamphlets, and writing material set neatly upon the table before her. In the midst of them were two framed photographs, which she polished one after another with a silken scarf that was near.

One of these was a picture of her father, who looked like an Englishman, with his clean-shaved mouth and chin, and closely-cropped side-whiskers, just turning grey. A good-humored shrewdness shone in his eyes. From the set of his thin, firm lips one might guess that he was in the foremost rank in the interesting game of "push" that occupies mankind. One might further guess that his cleverness in using opportunities had brought him there, and that a dexterous management of elbows had served him no less. The other picture was that of Georgie's fiancé, Mr. Meredith Holt, approaching more closely than he liked to his forty-fifth year and an unbecoming corpulence. Only one who knew beforehand that he was a *viveur* could have detected evidence of such in his face, which told little more than that he was a good-looking and amiable man of the world, who might be counted on to do the gentlemanly thing always. Georgie was going to marry him because his personality pleased her; because his easy knowledge of life – such as she apprehended it – commended itself to her approval; because he was likely to interfere in no way with her "work". Yet she might not have given any of these reasons if asked for one. Mr. Meredith Holt was simply an eligible man, whom almost any girl in her set would have accepted for a husband.

Georgie had just discovered that she had yet an hour to spare before starting out with the committee of four to further investigate the moral condition of the factory-girl, when a maid appeared with the announcement that a person was below who wished to see her.

"A person? Surely not a visitor at this hour?"

"I left her in the hall, miss, and she says her name is Mademoiselle Sal-Sal-"

"Oh, yes! Ask her to kindly walk up to my room, and show her the way, please, Hannah."

Mademoiselle Salambre came in with a sweep of skirts that bristled defiance, and a poise of the head that was aggressive in its backward tilt. She seated herself, and with an air of challenge waited to be questioned or addressed.

Georgie felt at ease amid her own familiar surroundings. While she made some idle tracings with a pencil upon a discarded envelope, she half turned to say:

"This visit of yours is very surprising, madam, and wholly useless. I suppose you guess my motive in recalling my work, as I have done."

"Maybe I do, and maybe I do not, Mees McEndairs," replied the woman, with an impertinent uplifting of the eyebrows.

Georgie felt the same shrinking which had overtaken her before in the woman's presence. But she knew her duty, and from that there was no shrinking.

"You must be made to understand, madam, that there is a right way to live, and that there is a wrong way," said Georgie with more condescension than she knew. "We cannot defy God's laws with impunity, and without incurring His displeasure. But in His infinite justice and mercy He offers forgiveness, love and protection to those who turn away from evil and repent. It is for each of us to follow the divine way as well as may be. And I am only humbly striving to do His will."

"A most charming sermon, Mees McEndairs!" mademoiselle interrupted with a nervous laugh; "it seems a great pity to waste it upon so small an audience. And it grieves me, I cannot express, that I have not the time to remain and listen to its close."

She arose and began to talk volubly, swiftly, in a jumble of French and English, and with a wealth of expression and gesture which Georgie could hardly believe was natural, and not something acquired and rehearsed.

She had come to inform Miss McEnders that she did not want her work; that she would not touch it with the tips of her fingers. And her little, gloved hands recoiled from an imaginary pile of lingerie with unspeakable disgust. Her eyes had traveled nimbly over the room, and had been arrested by the two photographs on the table. Very small, indeed, were her worldly possessions, she informed the young lady; but as Heaven was her witness – not a mouthful of bread that she had not earned. And her parents over yonder in France! As honest as the sunlight! Poor, ah! For that – poor as rats. God only knew how poor; and God only knew how honest. Her eyes remained fixed upon the picture of Horace McEnders. Some people might like fine houses, and servants, and horses, and all the luxury which dishonest wealth brings. Some people might enjoy such surroundings. As for her! – and she drew up her skirts ever so carefully and daintily, as though she feared contamination to her petticoats from the touch of the rich rug upon which she stood.

Georgie's blue eyes were filled with astonishment as they followed the woman's gestures. Her face showed aversion and perplexity.

"Please let this interview come to an end at once," spoke the girl. She would not deign to ask an explanation of the mysterious allusions to ill-gotten wealth. But mademoiselle had not yet said all that she had come there to say.

"If it was only me to say so," she went on, still looking at the likeness, "but, *cher maître!* Go, yourself Mees McEndairs, and stand for a while on the street and ask the people passing by how your dear papa has made his money, and see what they will say."

Then shifting her glance to the photograph of Meredith Holt, she stood in an attitude of amused contemplation, with a smile of commiseration playing about her lips.

"Mr. Meredith Holt!" she pronounced with quiet suppressed emphasis – "ah! *C'est un propre, celui la!* You know him very well, no doubt, Mees McEndairs. You would not care to have my opinion of

Mr. Meredith Holt. It would make no difference to you, Mees McEndairs, to know that he is not fit to be the husband of a self-respecting bar-maid. Oh! You know a good deal, my dear young lady. You can preach sermons in *merveille!*"

When Georgie was finally alone, there came to her, through all her disgust and indignation, an indefinable uneasiness. There was no misunderstanding the intention of the woman's utterances in regard to the girl's fiancé and her father. A sudden, wild, defiant desire came to her to test the suggestion which Mademoiselle Salambre had let fall.

Yes, she would go stand there on the corner and ask the passers-by how Horace McEnders made his money. She could not yet collect her thoughts for calm reflection; and the house stifled her. It was fully time for her to join her committee of four, but she would meddle no further with morals till her own were adjusted, she thought. Then she quitted the house, very pale, even to her lips that were tightly set.

Georgie stationed herself on the opposite side of the street, on the corner, and waited there as though she had appointed to meet some one.

The first to approach her was a kind-looking old gentleman, very much muffled for the pleasant spring day. Georgie did not hesitate an instant to accost him:

"I beg pardon, sir. Will you kindly tell me whose house that is?" pointing to her own domicile across the way.

"That is Mr. Horace McEnders' residence, Madam," replied the old gentleman, lifting his hat politely.

"Could you tell me how he made the money with which to build so magnificent a home?"

"You should not ask indiscreet questions, my dear young lady," answered the mystified old gentleman, as he bowed and walked away.

The girl let one or two persons pass her. Then she stopped a plumber, who was going cheerily along with his bag of tools on his shoulder.

"I beg pardon," began Georgie again; "but may I ask whose residence that is across the street?"

"Yes'um. That's the McEnderses."

"Thank you; and can you tell me how Mr. McEnders made such an immense fortune?"

"Oh, that ain't my business; but they say he made the biggest pile of it in the Whisky Ring."

So the truth would come to her somehow! These were the people from whom to seek it – who had not learned to veil their thoughts and opinions in polite subterfuge.

When a careless little news-boy came strolling along, she stopped him with the apparent intention of buying a paper from him.

"Do you know whose house that is?" she asked him, handing him a piece of money and nodding over the way.

"W'y, dats ole MicAndrus' house."

"I wonder where he got the money to build such a fine house."

"He stole it. Dats where he got it. Thank you," pocketing the change which Georgie declined to take, and he whistled a popular air as he disappeared around the corner.

Georgie had heard enough. Her heart was beating violently now, and her cheeks were flaming. So everybody knew it; even to the street gamins! The men and women who visited her and broke bread at her father's table, knew it. Her coworkers, who strove with her in Christian endeavor, knew. The very servants who waited upon her doubtless knew this, and had their jests about it.

She shrank within herself as she climbed the stairway to her room.

Upon the table there she found a box of exquisite white spring blossoms that a messenger had brought from Meredith Holt, during her absence. Without an instant's hesitation, Georgie cast the spotless things into the wide, sooty, fireplace. Then she sank into a chair and wept bitterly.

The Blind Man

Originally appeared in *Vogue*, 13 May 1897

A man carrying a small red box in one hand walked slowly down the street. His old straw hat and faded garments looked as if the rain had often beaten upon them, and the sun had as many times dried them upon his person. He was not old, but he seemed feeble; and he walked in the sun, along the blistering asphalt pavement. On the opposite side of the street there were trees that threw a thick and pleasant shade: people were all walking on that side. But the man did not know, for he was blind, and moreover he was stupid.

In the red box were lead pencils, which he was endeavoring to sell. He carried no stick, but guided himself by trailing his foot along the stone copings or his hand along the iron railings. When he came to the steps of a house he would mount them. Sometimes, after reaching the door with great difficulty, he could not find the electric button, whereupon he would patiently descend and go his way. Some of the iron gates were locked, their owners being away for the summer, and he would consume much time striving to open them, which made little difference, as he had all the time there was at his disposal.

At times he succeeded in finding the electric button: but the man or maid who answered the bell needed no pencil, nor could they be induced to disturb the mistress of the house about so small a thing.

The man had been out long and had walked far, but had sold nothing. That morning someone who had finally grown tired of having him hanging around had equipped him with this box of pencils, and sent him out to make his living. Hunger, with sharp fangs, was gnawing at his stomach and a consuming thirst parched his mouth and tortured him. The sun was broiling. He wore too much clothing—a vest and coat over his shirt. He might have removed these and carried them on his arm or thrown them away; but he did not think of it. A kind woman who saw him from an upper window felt sorry for him, and wished that he would cross over into the shade.

The man drifted into a side street, where there was a group of noisy, excited children at play. The color of the box which he carried attracted them and they wanted to know what was in it. One of them attempted to take it away from him. With the instinct to protect his own and his only means of sustenance, he resisted, shouted at the children and called them names. A policeman coming round the corner and seeing that he was the centre of a disturbance, jerked him violently around by the collar; but upon perceiving that he was blind, considerably refrained from clubbing him and sent him on his way. He walked on in the sun.

During his aimless rambling he turned into a street where there were monster electric cars thundering up and down, clanging wild bells and literally shaking the ground beneath his feet with their terrific impetus. He started to cross the street.

Then something happened—something horrible happened that made the women faint and the strongest men who saw it grow sick and dizzy. The motorman's lips were as gray as his face, and that was ashen gray; and he shook and staggered from the superhuman effort he had put forth to stop his car.

Where could the crowds have come from so suddenly,as if by magic? Boys on the run, men and women tearing up on their wheels to see the sickening sight: doctors dashing up in buggies as if directed by Providence.

And the horror grew when the multitude recognized in the dead and mangled figure one of the wealthiest, most useful and most influential men of the town, a man noted for his prudence and foresight. How could such a terrible fate have overtaken him? He was hastening from his business house, for he was late, to join his family, who were to start in an hour or two for their summer home on the Atlantic coast. In his hurry he did not perceive the other car coming from the opposite direction and the common, harrowing thing was repeated.

The blind man did not know what the commotion was all about. He had crossed the street, and there he was, stumbling on in the sun, trailing his foot along the coping.

The Kiss

Originally appeared in Vogue, 17 Jan 1895

It was still quite light out of doors, but inside with the curtains drawn and the smouldering fire sending out a dim, uncertain glow, the room was full of deep shadows.

Brantain sat in one of these shadows; it had overtaken him and he did not mind. The obscurity lent him courage to keep his eyes fastened as ardently as he liked upon the girl who sat in the firelight.

She was very handsome, with a certain fine, rich coloring that belongs to the healthy brune type. She was quite composed, as she idly stroked the satiny coat of the cat that lay curled in her lap, and she occasionally sent a slow glance into the shadow where her companion sat. They were talking low, of indifferent things which plainly were not the things that occupied their thoughts. She knew that he loved her – a frank, blustering fellow without guile enough to conceal his feelings, and no desire to do so. For two weeks past he had sought her society eagerly and persistently. She was confidently waiting for him to declare himself and she meant to accept him. The rather insignificant and unattractive Brantain was enormously rich; and she liked and required the entourage which wealth could give her.

During one of the pauses between their talk of the last tea and the next reception the door opened and a young man entered whom Brantain knew quite well. The girl turned her face toward him. A stride or two brought him to her side, and bending over her chair – before she could suspect his intention, for she did not realize that he had not seen her visitor – he pressed an ardent, lingering kiss upon her lips.

Brantain slowly arose; so did the girl arise, but quickly, and the newcomer stood between them, a little amusement and some defiance struggling with the confusion in his face.

"I believe," stammered Brantain, "I see that I have stayed too long. I – I had no idea – that is, I must wish you good-by." He was clutching his hat with both hands, and probably did not perceive that she was extending her hand to him, her presence of mind had not completely deserted her; but she could not have trusted herself to speak.

"Hang me if I saw him sitting there, Nattie! I know it's deuced awkward for you. But I hope you'll forgive me this once – this very first break. Why, what's the matter?"

"Don't touch me; don't come near me," she returned angrily. "What do you mean by entering the house without ringing?"

"I came in with your brother, as I often do," he answered coldly, in self-justification. "We came in the side way. He went upstairs and I came in here hoping to find you. The explanation is simple enough and ought to satisfy you that the misadventure was unavoidable. But do say that you forgive me, Nathalie," he entreated, softening.

"Forgive you! You don't know what you are talking about. Let me pass. It depends upon – a good deal whether I ever forgive you."

At that next reception which she and Brantain had been talking about she approached the young man with a delicious frankness of manner when she saw him there.

"Will you let me speak to you a moment or two, Mr. Brantain?" she asked with an engaging but perturbed smile. He seemed extremely unhappy; but when she took his arm and walked away with him, seeking a retired corner, a ray of hope mingled with the almost comical misery of his expression. She was apparently very outspoken.

"Perhaps I should not have sought this interview, Mr. Brantain; but – but, oh, I have been very uncomfortable, almost miserable since that little encounter the other afternoon. When I thought how you might have misinterpreted it, and believed things" – hope was plainly gaining the ascendancy over misery in Brantain's round guileless face – "of course, I know it is nothing to you, but for my own sake I do want you to understand that Mr. Harvy is an intimate friend of long standing. Why, we have always been like cousins – like brother and sister, I may say. He is my brother's most intimate associate and often fancies that he is entitled to the same privileges as the family. Oh, I know it is absurd, uncalled for, to tell you this; undignified even," she was almost weeping, "but it makes so much difference to me what you think of – of me." Her voice had grown very low and agitated. The misery had all disappeared from Brantain's face.

"Then you do really care what I think, Miss Nathalie? May I call you Miss Nathalie?" They turned into a long, dim corridor that was lined on either side with tall, graceful plants. They walked slowly to the very end of it. When they turned to retrace their steps Brantain's face was radiant and hers was triumphant.

****

Harvy was among the guests at the wedding; and he sought her out in a rare moment when she stood alone.

"Your husband," he said, smiling, "has sent me over to kiss you."

A quick blush suffused her face and round polished throat. "I suppose it's natural for a man to feel and act generously on an occasion of this kind. He tells me he doesn't want his marriage to interrupt wholly that pleasant intimacy which has existed between you and me. I don't know what you've been telling him," with an insolent smile, "but he has sent me here to kiss you."

She felt like a chess player who, by the clever handling of his pieces, sees the game taking the course intended. Her eyes were bright and tender with a smile as they glanced up into his; and her lips looked hungry for the kiss which they invited.

"But, you know," he went on quietly, "I didn't tell him so, it would have seemed ungrateful, but I can tell you. I've stopped kissing women; it's dangerous."

Well, she had Brantain and his million left. A person can't have everything in this world; and it was a little unreasonable of her to expect it.

The Locket

I

One night in autumn a few men were gathered about a fire on the slope of a hill. They belonged to a small detachment of Confederate forces and were awaiting orders to march. Their gray uniforms were worn beyond the point of shabbiness. One of the men was heating something in a tin cup over the embers. Two were lying at full length a little distance away, while a fourth was trying to decipher a letter and had drawn close to the light. He had unfastened his collar and a good bit of his flannel shirt front.

"What's that you got around your neck, Ned?" asked one of the men lying in the obscurity.

Ned—or Edmond—mechanically fastened another button of his shirt and did not reply. He went on reading his letter.

"Is it your sweet heart's picture?"

"'Taint no gal's picture," offered the man at the fire. He had removed his tin cup and was engaged in stirring its grimy contents with a small stick. "That's a charm; some kind of hoodoo business that one o' them priests gave him to keep him out o' trouble. I know them Cath'lics. That's how come Frenchy got permoted an never got a scratch sence he's been in the ranks. Hey, French! aint I right?" Edmond looked up absently from his letter.

"What is it?" he asked.

"Aint that a charm you got round your neck?"

"It must be, Nick," returned Edmond with a smile. "I don't know how I could have gone through this year and a half without it."

The letter had made Edmond heart sick and home sick. He stretched himself on his back and looked straight up at the blinking stars. But he was not thinking of them nor of anything but a certain spring day when the bees were humming in the clematis; when a girl was saying good bye to him. He could see her as she unclasped from her neck the locket which she fastened about his own. It was an old fashioned golden locket bearing miniatures of her father and mother with their names and the date of their marriage. It was her most precious earthly possession. Edmond could feel again the folds of the girl's soft white gown, and see the droop of the angel-sleeves as she circled her fair arms about his neck. Her sweet face, appealing, pathetic, tormented by the pain of parting, appeared before him as vividly as life. He turned over, burying his face in his arm and there he lay, still and motionless.

The profound and treacherous night with its silence and semblance of peace settled upon the camp. He dreamed that the fair Octavie brought him a letter. He had no chair to offer her and was pained and embarrassed at the condition of his garments. He was ashamed of the poor food which comprised the dinner at which he begged her to join them.

He dreamt of a serpent coiling around his throat, and when he strove to grasp it the slimy thing glided away from his clutch. Then his dream was clamor.

"Git your duds! you! Frenchy!" Nick was bellowing in his face. There was what appeared to be a scramble and a rush rather than any regulated movement. The hill side was alive with clatter and motion; with sudden up-springing lights among the pines. In the east the dawn was unfolding out of the darkness. Its glimmer was yet dim in the plain below.

"What's it all about?" wondered a big black bird perched in the top of the tallest tree. He was an old solitary and a wise one, yet he was not wise enough to guess what it was all about. So all day long he kept blinking and wondering.

The noise reached far out over the plain and across the hills and awoke the little babes that were sleeping in their cradles. The smoke curled up toward the sun and shadowed the plain so that the stupid birds thought it was going to rain; but the wise one knew better.

"They are children playing a game," thought he. "I shall know more about it if I watch long enough."

At the approach of night they had all vanished away with their din and smoke. Then the old bird plumed his feathers. At last he had understood! With a flap of his great, black wings he shot downward, circling toward the plain.

A man was picking his way across the plain. He was dressed in the garb of a clergyman. His mission was to administer the consolations of religion to any of the prostrate figures in whom there might yet linger a spark of life. A negro accompanied him, bearing a bucket of water and a flask of wine.

There were no wounded here; they had been borne away. But the retreat had been hurried and the vultures and the good Samaritans would have to look to the dead.

There was a soldier—a mere boy—lying with his face to the sky. His hands were clutching the sward on either side and his finger nails were stuffed with earth and bits of grass that he had gathered in his despairing grasp upon life. His musket was gone; he was hatless and his face and clothing were begrimed. Around his neck hung a gold chain and locket. The priest, bending over him, unclasped the chain and removed it from the dead soldier's neck. He had grown used to the terrors of war and could face them unflinchingly; but its pathos, someway, always brought the tears to his old, dim eyes.

The angelus was ringing half a mile away. The priest and the negro knelt and murmured together the evening benediction and a prayer for the dead.

II

The peace and beauty of a spring day had descended upon the earth like a benediction. Along the leafy road which skirted a narrow, tortuous stream in central Louisiana, rumbled an old fashioned cabriolet, much the worse for hard and rough usage over country roads and lanes. The fat, black horses went in a slow, measured trot, notwithstanding constant urging on the part of the fat, black coachman. Within the vehicle were seated the fair Octavie and her old friend and neighbor, Judge Pillier, who had come to take her for a morning drive.

103

Octavie wore a plain black dress, severe in its simplicity. A narrow belt held it at the waist and the sleeves were gathered into close fitting wristbands. She had discarded her hoopskirt and appeared not unlike a nun. Beneath the folds of her bodice nestled the old locket. She never displayed it now. It had returned to her sanctified in her eyes; made precious as material things sometimes are by being forever identified with a significant moment of one's existence.

A hundred times she had read over the letter with which the locket had come back to her. No later than that morning she had again pored over it. As she sat beside the window, smoothing the letter out upon her knee, heavy and spiced odors stole in to her with the songs of birds and the humming of insects in the air.

She was so young and the world was so beautiful that there came over her a sense of unreality as she read again and again the priest's letter. He told of that autumn day drawing to its close, with the gold and the red fading out of the west, and the night gathering its shadows to cover the faces of the dead. Oh! She could not believe that one of those dead was her own! with visage uplifted to the gray sky in an agony of supplication. A spasm of resistance and rebellion seized and swept over her. Why was the spring here with its flowers and its seductive breath if he was dead! Why was she here! What further had she to do with life and the living!

Octavie had experienced many such moments of despair, but a blessed resignation had never failed to follow, and it fell then upon her like a mantle and enveloped her.

"I shall grow old and quiet and sad like poor Aunt Tavie," she murmured to herself as she folded the letter and replaced it in the secretary. Already she gave herself a little demure air like her Aunt Tavie. She walked with a slow glide in unconscious imitation of Mademoiselle Tavie whom some youthful affliction had robbed of earthly compensation while leaving her in possession of youth's illusions.

As she sat in the old cabriolet beside the father of her dead lover, again there came to Octavie the terrible sense of loss which had assailed her so often before. The soul of her youth clamored for its rights; for a share in the world's glory and exultation. She leaned back and drew her veil a little closer about her face. It was an old black veil of her Aunt Tavie's. A whiff of dust from the road had blown in and she wiped her cheeks and her eyes with her soft, white handkerchief, a homemade handkerchief, fabricated from one of her old fine muslin petticoats.

"Will you do me the favor, Octavie," requested the judge in the courteous tone which he never abandoned, "to remove that veil which you wear. It seems out of harmony, someway, with the beauty and promise of the day."

The young girl obediently yielded to her old companion's wish and unpinning the cumbersome, sombre drapery from her bonnet, folded it neatly and laid it upon the seat in front of her.

"Ah! that is better; far better!" he said in a tone expressing unbounded relief. "Never put it on again, dear." Octavie felt a little hurt; as if he wished to debar her from share and parcel in the burden of affliction which had been placed upon all of them. Again she drew forth the old muslin handkerchief.

They had left the big road and turned into a level plain which had formerly been an old meadow. There were clumps of thorn trees here and there, gorgeous in their spring radiance. Some cattle were grazing off in the distance in spots where the grass was tall and luscious. At the far end of the meadow was the towering lilac hedge, skirting the lane that led to Judge Pillier's house, and the scent of its heavy blossoms met them like a soft and tender embrace of welcome.

As they neared the house the old gentleman placed an arm around the girl's shoulders and turning her face up to him he said: "Do you not think that on a day like this, miracles might happen? When the whole earth is vibrant with life, does it not seem to you, Octavie, that heaven might for once relent and give us back our dead?" He spoke very low, advisedly, and impressively. In his voice was an old quaver which was not habitual and there was agitation in every line of his visage. She gazed at him with eyes that were full of supplication and a certain terror of joy.

They had been driving through the lane with the towering hedge on one side and the open meadow on the other. The horses had somewhat quickened their lazy pace. As they turned into the avenue leading to the house, a whole choir of feathered songsters fluted a sudden torrent of melodious greeting from their leafy hiding places.

Octavie felt as if she had passed into a stage of existence which was like a dream, more poignant and real than life. There was the old gray house with its sloping eaves. Amid the blur of green, and dimly, she saw familiar faces and heard voices as if they came from far across the fields, and Edmond was holding her. Her dead Edmond; her living Edmond, and she felt the beating of his heart against her and the agonizing rapture of his kisses striving to awake her. It was as if the spirit of life and the awakening spring had given back the soul to her youth and bade her rejoice.

It was many hours later that Octavie drew the locket from her bosom and looked at Edmond with a questioning appeal in her glance.

"It was the night before an engagement," he said. "In the hurry of the encounter, and the retreat next day, I never missed it till the fight was over. I thought of course I had lost it in the heat of the struggle, but it was stolen."

"Stolen," she shuddered, and thought of the dead soldier with his face uplifted to the sky in an agony of supplication.

Edmond said nothing; but he thought of his messmate; the one who had lain far back in the shadow; the one who had said nothing.

The Night Came Slowly

Originally appeared in Moods, July 1895

I am losing my interest in human beings; in the significance of their lives and their actions. Some one has said it is better to study one man than ten books. I want neither books nor men; they make me suffer. Can one of them talk to me like the night – the Summer night? Like the stars or the caressing wind?

The night came slowly, softly, as I lay out there under the maple tree. It came creeping, creeping stealthily out of the valley, thinking I did not notice. And the outlines of trees and foliage nearby blended in one black mass and the night came stealing out from them, too, and from the east and west, until the only light was in the sky, filtering through the maple leaves and a star looking down through every cranny.

The night is solemn and it means mystery.

Human shapes flitted by like intangible things. Some stole up like little mice to peep at me. I did not mind. My whole being was abandoned to the soothing and penetrating charm of the night.

The katydids began their slumber song: they are at it yet. How wise they are. They do not chatter like people. They tell me only: "sleep, sleep, sleep." The wind rippled the maple leaves like little warm love thrills.

Why do fools cumber the Earth! It was a man's voice that broke the necromancer's spell. A man came to-day with his "Bible Class." He is detestable with his red cheeks and bold eyes and coarse manner and speech. What does he know of Christ? Shall I ask a young fool who was born yesterday and will die tomorrow to tell me things of Christ? I would rather ask the stars: they have seen him.

The Story of an Hour

Originally appear in *Vogue*, 6 December 1894

Knowing that Mrs. Mallard was afflicted with a heart trouble, great care was taken to break to her as gently as possible the news of her husband's death.

It was her sister Josephine who told her, in broken sentences; veiled hints that revealed in half concealing. Her husband's friend Richards was there, too, near her. It was he who had been in the newspaper office when intelligence of the railroad disaster was received, with Brently Mallard's name leading the list of "killed." He had only taken the time to assure himself of its truth by a second telegram, and had hastened to forestall any less careful, less tender friend in bearing the sad message.

She did not hear the story as many women have heard the same, with a paralyzed inability to accept its significance. She wept at once, with sudden, wild abandonment, in her sister's arms. When the storm of grief had spent itself she went away to her room alone. She would have no one follow her.

There stood, facing the open window, a comfortable, roomy armchair. Into this she sank, pressed down by a physical exhaustion that haunted her body and seemed to reach into her soul.

She could see in the open square before her house the tops of trees that were all aquiver with the new spring life. The delicious breath of rain was in the air. In the street below a peddler was crying his wares. The notes of a distant song which some one was singing reached her faintly, and countless sparrows were twittering in the eaves. There were patches of blue sky showing here and there through the clouds that had met and piled one above the other in the west facing her window.

She sat with her head thrown back upon the cushion of the chair, quite motionless, except when a sob came up into her throat and shook her, as a child who has cried itself to sleep continues to sob in its dreams.

She was young, with a fair, calm face, whose lines bespoke repression and even a certain strength. But now there was a dull stare in her eyes, whose gaze was fixed away off yonder on one of those patches of blue sky. It was not a glance of reflection, but rather indicated a suspension of intelligent thought.

There was something coming to her and she was waiting for it, fearfully. What was it? She did not know; it was too subtle and elusive to name. But she felt it, creeping out of the sky, reaching toward her through the sounds, the scents, the color that filled the air.

Now her bosom rose and fell tumultuously. She was beginning to recognize this thing that was approaching to possess her, and she was striving to beat it back with her will—as powerless as her two white slender hands would have been. When she abandoned herself a little whispered word escaped her slightly parted lips. She said it over and over under her breath: "free, free, free!" The vacant stare and the look of terror that had followed it went from her eyes. They stayed keen and bright. Her pulses beat fast, and the coursing blood warmed and relaxed every inch of her body. She did not stop to ask if it were or were not a monstrous joy that held her. A clear and exalted perception enabled her to dismiss the suggestion as trivial.

She knew that she would weep again when she saw the kind, tender hands folded in death; the face that had never looked save with love upon her, fixed and gray and dead. But she saw beyond that bitter moment a long procession of years to come that would belong to her absolutely. And she opened and spread her arms out to them in welcome. There would be no one to live for during those coming years; she would live for herself. There would be no powerful will bending hers in that blind persistence with which men and women believe they have a right to impose a private will upon a fellow-creature. A kind intention or a cruel intention made the act seem no less a crime as she looked upon it in that brief moment of illumination.

And yet she had loved him—sometimes. Often she had not. What did it matter! What could love, the unsolved mystery, count for in face of this possession of self-assertion which she suddenly recognized as the strongest impulse of her being!

"Free! Body and soul free!" she kept whispering.

Josephine was kneeling before the closed door with her lips to the keyhole, imploring for admission. "Louise, open the door! I beg, open the door—you will make yourself ill. What are you doing, Louise? For heaven's sake open the door."

"Go away. I am not making myself ill." No; she was drinking in a very elixir of life through that open window. Her fancy was running riot along those days ahead of her. Spring days, and summer days, and all sorts of days that would be her own. She breathed a quick prayer that life might be long. It was only yesterday she had thought with a shudder that life might be long.

She arose at length and opened the door to her sister's importunities. There was a feverish triumph in her eyes, and she carried herself unwittingly like a goddess of Victory. She clasped her sister's waist, and together they descended the stairs. Richards stood waiting for them at the bottom.

Someone was opening the front door with a latchkey. It was Brently Mallard who entered, a little travel-stained, composedly carrying his grip-sack and umbrella. He had been far from the scene of the accident, and did not even know there had been one. He stood amazed at Josephine's piercing cry; at Richards' quick motion to screen him from the view of his wife.

But Richards was too late.

When the doctors came they said she had died of heart disease — of the joy that kills.

COLCHESTER SIXTH FORM COLLEGE
LIBRARY

Printed in the United Kingdom by
Lightning Source UK Ltd., Milton Keynes
142408UK00002B/208/P